Praise for Fish Story Prize Shortlisted;
ScreenCraft Semifinalist
Loveoid

"*Loveoid* is a wildly unique and immensely realized science fiction thriller set in a dystopian present in which overpopulation is decimating the Earth and its natural resources at a rapid rate. Additionally, the world of the story is incredibly deep, filled with dense detail and nuance that give the impression of a very realized universe."

— *ScreenCraft*

"The smart choice to set this eco-thriller in the present brings home the tenebrous climate prognostications we usually reserve for another year."

— *Brussels Express*

"With a new, scary virus as the backdrop, Olivia and Khalid navigate love, cures, and a different world. A timely novel with an interesting message about love and nature."

— *Booklist*

"As overpopulation grows, natural resources are depleted, species go extinct, and the polar ice caps continue to melt. People now check into euthanasia hotels to escape a hopeless future.... The story's premise is interesting."

— *Library Journal*

"Morin's wit can be delicious."

— *Canberra Times*, Australia

"About time some serious writers and artists took on the biggest issue of our time — maybe all time. This story shows that engagement fully underway!"

— Bill McKibben, founder 350.org

"*Loveoid* is one of the most incredibly meaningful books I've read in recent times. Author J.L. Morin, very cleverly discusses so many topics in one story. We, being in a pandemic situation right now, can relate to the story so much. After reading this book, my faith in love is restored since I, too, believe that love is the cure for many ailments in this world."

— *The Clipped Nightingale*

"*Loveoid* is a rare and most accurate reflection of contemporary LGBTI people: I both love and find highly enlightening JL Morin's particular reference to the Navajo culture—it reminds me of the recent apology of Canadian Prime Minister Trudeau for suppressing the 'two-spirit Canadian Indigenous peoples' values and beliefs'. Many ancient cultures accepted non-binary people and it is important to be constantly reminded of this, given the current confusion, deliberate misunderstandings and hatred around this subject. Also, focusing on love (rather than sex which is primarily linked to re-production) is the perfect romantic, humane and noble premise."

— Dimitris Politis, author, LGBTI rights champion

"I take heart from JL Morin's ethereal intuition: true love is what eventually will separate man from vegetable."

— A. Bergsten, author, *The Rift*

"*Loveoid*, the new novel from JL Morin, aims to change the evolutionary trajectory of life on Earth by putting power into the hands of those who love rather than those who prey.... The often poetic narrative looks at life on a grand scale while also magnifying a story of unlikely lovers.... Most intriguing and satisfying are Morin's blending of Nature on Earth—light, shadow, sea turtle, snake, extinct species, and sandstorm—with self and ponderance. The author lifts the gaze of humans to what exists outside our walls and windows and establishes how these things shape and inspire us. Breathing life into ancient wisdom, *Loveoid* demonstrates how we might fit in with Nature, or get back to it. How we might preserve it before it's too late."

—*Dragonfly.eco*

"In *Loveoid*, J.L. Morin spins a tale of awakening and vision, a tale that has hopefulness in it but does not overdo the optimism. Morin writes with both passion and great intelligence, at ease with complex philosophical ideas. She is not afraid to tackle head-on the most pressing and dire issues of today, and she does so with focus, storytelling verve, and an admirable clarity."

—*DoSomeDamage.com*

Loveoid

JL Morin

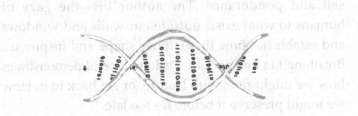

Harvard Square Editions
New York
2020

This story takes place in the present day.

Fact: The world has its first robot citizen, a milestone in the cessation of humankind's dominance over computers. Named Sophia, she was confirmed as a Saudi citizen in 2017 during a business event in Riyadh.

Fact: The ashram of the spiritual luminary Osho in Pune, India holds funeral celebrations to rejoice in the passage to the beyond. His promotion of euthanasia addressed the economic theory of the Malthusian Trap, that population growth inevitably correlates with diminishing returns as our exponentially growing populace outstrips resources. Osho was assassinated in 1990.

Fact: The Nazca lines are among archaeology's most puzzling mysteries. From before 1500 BCE, the lines depict living creatures, stylized plants, and mythical beings, but the most enigmatic discovery is the mountain tops. Scientists have said that the mysterious Nazca mountain tops look as if something shaved off the mountain peaks to render incredibly flat surfaces resembling modern runways.

Fact: Assisting suicide has been legal in Switzerland since the enlightenment. It became legal in in Germany in 2014, and in Victoria, Australia in 2019. Aid in dying statutes are in effect in the US states of Montana, California, Colorado, District of Columbia, Hawaii, Maine, New Jersey, Oregon, Vermont, Washington, and Washington DC. Euthanasia is legal in Belgium, Canada, Colombia, Luxembourg, and the Netherlands. Assisted dying services offer a basis for decision-making to shape life until the end as 'the last human right'.

Third Eye

Messages travel on waves. Radio waves are the lowest frequency of the seven waves in the known electromagnetic spectrum. Internet uses a frequency band between radio waves and microwaves. All matter emits waves.

IN DEEP MEDITATION where all resolves, Oneness sought awareness, and split to become duality.

Et tu? thought the woman in black. Even Oneness, to see itself in mirrors of relatedness, divided. Was life a betrayal of death then, or betrayal just an illusion as remorseless as breathing, another word for evolution; no need for indignance, every infraction merely clearing space for life's next spiral.

A peregrine feinted from its perch atop a lone pine and flapped its wings. The wind yawned, stopping the falcon midair. The woman in the black hijab shielded her eyes against the sun and watched the bird, frozen there. Where the infinite embodied itself in the finite. Bird halted in sky. The gust thrashed at the beach below, littered with death tourists.

Tilting its wings, the falcon wafted higher, feathers separating in the wind. Wouldn't that be something, to fly into this long inhalation of Unity's, as it expanded itself indefinitely before exhaling all back to singularity. You just inhaled, and from inspiration back to expiration, and from negative to positive, no longer thinking in one direction. Life doubted Oneness. It believed in two, moving dialectically from one pole to its opposite, out warm air, in cool, quieting your inner dialogue, till you became your breath.

A favorable crosscurrent carried the bird out to sea, where it circled in hunt of energy. *Predators at the top love the least.* The thought flew across her mind, before a strange experience.

As if the wind strummed up a trinity, she was suddenly looking down at her own body standing on the cliff, next to the man in the khaki shorts. And strikingly, the man, dressed as trendily as a store window (in signature button-down shirt and red tie flapping in the wind), like a mannequin, had no head. He walked right by without taking notice of her.

She was sure now: he couldn't see her, or anything else; she shouldn't take it personally. Did she speak out loud? because the man responded, jarring her back into her body.

"Love!" He turned around to look at her in her hijab, standing there presently. "We can hardly block the masses from coming to the euthanasia hotel."

He hadn't seen the falcon. Axel hadn't seen a lot of things.

She was also in denial, about her out-of-body experience, already putting it down to the conductivity of copper deposits in the red soil, which did have something to do with it. She could, feel a remarkable energy coiling through her, though, looking at the chest of the seven-foot man. Suspecting his blindness might reveal the missing puzzle piece, she raised her gaze to his neck, to the razor stubble on his jaw, his head there now...

He was scratching his chin. "And why should we? Extinction levels are a thousand times higher because of humans."

The bird soared above a small flock of Dalmatian pelicans, one of hundreds of local species becoming extinct. The pelicans flew through the pageantry of creation as if sharing one mind. The falcon circled twice. Then it pulled its wings into a teardrop.

The woman peered through black sunglasses. "Oh no!" The saliva in her mouth dried up.

The man turned around. "A falcon! It's going to attack."

The predator shot through the azure at a velocity of 200 miles per hour, transparent third eyelid wiping its cornea to maintain moisture as it locked onto its prey. The falcon hit the pelican. The impact sent the fowl spinning, its webbed feet paddling the air in an orchestra of flapping. The awkward freefall ceased. The pelican toppled onto the shallow waves. Life crashed on the beach.

Involvement with finitude consummate, the absolute returned to infinity.

Her breathing had stopped on the exhale, adrenaline coursing.

Elderly bathers emerged from the sea and collapsed on their striped divans. Under shut eyelids, they warmed their dormant genes and dreamt of a world that had forgotten how to hunt, death (and life) sanitized out of existence, and didn't see the falcon's claws extend eight scythes to retrieve the pelican carcass and fly it down the shore, shadow rippling across the cliff face.

Feeling like a detective uncovering an important clue, she beheld this shard of mirror from her mind's eye.

Crickets cajoled, their mating cacophony drowning out the beach-bar radio and leaving the humans on their divans with their naked dilemma, *that the loving don't survive.*

Wargames

On the waves of Rising Sun FM — Karaoke is bad for your health, a Hong Kong study has found. No one wants the germs from your version of the hits.

THE PILOT gunned the power over Tokyo's Peninsula Hotel. Nose pointed into the wind, he prepared for vertical descent. Three minutes later, the CEO of Trident Fuel was walking across the helipad at a brisk pace to the elevator.

The other international delegates from disparate sectors were already out of their trench coats and into the stream of corporate consciousness. Trident's CEO ordered his double espresso from the sprightly attendant at the coffee cart, then lingered while everyone waited. Luther Ainsworth's swift maneuvering through a series of cold and conventional wars had grown Trident Fuel Company from 900 billion into a multi-trillion-dollar player. To say he had a high-profile job was a euphemism. His private fleet of jets and helicopters enabled him to give orders anywhere face-to-face on a spectrum of world-shaping issues. But he still managed to keep up his fascination with women. They offered a flavor of warfare requiring Gordian counter-plotting, frontline technology, and improvisational deceit to effectually undermine their prying, security, and emotional blackmail.

He handed his bomber jacket to the attendant. There was a measure of posturing before wrinkled hands would flip through photocopies. Still mystified by the item that had worked its way up to the top of the agenda, men of importance from top corporations worldwide needed time to congeal. Luther launched into a lengthy humblebrag on forgetting to send flowers to his mistress when he paid her hospital bill.

"What's she getting?" asked his colleague Shalom, of the Shalom Armaments dynasty.

"Abdominal liposuction."

"*Ja*. That is *gut*."

"Isn't it?"

"You work on your relationship."

Survival of the Meanest

Desert-FM — Humans are exterminating animal and plant species we depend on so quickly that scientists are observing an acceleration in mutations to keep up.

THIS EVOLUTIONARY PUZZLE always stumped the woman in the black hijab. Why should those who love least rise to the top? "Surely love isn't a weakness," she ventured out loud, as if she could rely on a colleague from the euthanasia hotel.

Presenting a slender torso, Axel placed one foot on a rock. He ran his hand over his golden-gray crew cut and peered down at her. The glint in his eyes recaptured the sun, and she was falling into the blue. The Mediterranean swelled to the horizon. A thin line divided a sky of possibility from the turning planet. The sea, languid, a dark blue stripe where the wind whipped the water. "A religious question, Dr. Murchadha."

Dismissed. The gleam in Axel's eye gone now, replaced by a mischievous smirk. She was a casual thought left on the cliff. Her headscarf fluttered. "A scientific question. It's the reason I went into biology! I studied—"

"I know," his voice authoritative with the British

accent, one blue eye open wide, the other relaxed, so close now, she could smell him. She took in his angular features and prominent nose. The waves below crashed on the shore with its death tourists. "You studied those shrimp that change sexes." He made it sound trite. *His blindness.*

"Only under environmental duress —"

"What was it called, 'Survival of the Sweetest'?"

A fishhook of a question.

"It's a viable hypothesis," scratching his razor stubble, "parthenogenesis caused by a lack of males."

"That was one of the assumptions."

He held her in dubious regard. "But you did suggest that humans are evolving into an asexual species," draining her energy.

"It was about developing a loveoid to let the loving survive." There was no need for further explanation, not after the kakistocracy's icy reception of her love experiment. Axel knew very well that disease struck the ones who refused to vent their stress. He'd done a study showing the gentlest died of cancer, and he also knew her experiment had worked in the short run. He'd taken pictures of her pack of foxes cuddled up with her litter of rabbits.

But he only circulated the pictures taken of Fluffy and Cotton after the chemical suddenly wore off. She could still see their bunny fuzz caught between the blades of grass. To rub it in, her colleagues spread rumors. No doubt he was setting her up for another one of his pranks. He wanted to hear her say she had no desire to have a baby by herself. Far be it from Olivia to convince scientists about love. Look where it had gotten her with Axel Harrington. Erased from his grant applications. While she was still writing the spiritual thug into hers. Well, she finally figured it out and crossed him off. Their relationship boiled down to cheap competition. She was dancing alone.

His long body balanced past her from foot to foot, button-down shirt rolled up at the sleeves, red tie flapping over his shoulder. The North African sun beat down undeniably. Sand lashed at her sunglasses as she followed his long strides away from the cliff. He had a perfect ass.

*

As they approached the other biologists, the men's bravado clamored to a halt.

Her features remained placid; if her position had been suppressed, so be it.

The senior epidemiologist, Faucheux, in his vest full of pockets said to her, "Have you found any interesting organ donors, *Docteur?*" The signal. Despite her scarf, the only woman was fair game.

Their chubby Aussie post-doc picked up this info filtering down from the apex, and jabbed next. "No need for other humans, then?"

"A dire need for human organs, though," Faucheux cackled.

She glared at the post-doc, who blushed, then pretended not to notice.

A prickly pear cast a black shadow on the cliff. Whatever reason they'd give for firing her, it wouldn't be the real one. Spiny fruits lay on the red Earth above the beach with its elderly bodies waiting to die. Her voice was steady, "I'll be the first to admit that ending human lives is the downside of the job."

"Better than to watch them starve," said the post-doc.

"The sun bounced off Faucheux's bald head. "Don't you worry, even after we kill off our own food supply, this operation will continue."

Not if they keep on promoting monads, she didn't say, and couldn't figure out why they were all stunned, as if a door had slammed. They were actually waiting for Axel to mediate.

He moved his body between her and Faucheux. "In the future, meaning now, the trend will be toward euthanasia hotels."

Everyone nodded, remembering United Nations Resolution 254, *Noting with concern the situation in desertified territories with foreign countries occupying land...* It had been a discreet revolution. Not a line in the newspapers about euthanasia facilities, and look at the demand. Still, the business conditions to attract normal investors did not exist here. Only one risk taker had an appetite for converting hotels to facilities in an area occupied by foreign troops. Once the rule of law was agreed on, their first-mover advantage would expire, and demand would bring in competition.

Axel took a firm stance, and tried to paint a motivating picture. "Marry tourism with euthanasia, and you've got a noble cause." He remained thankful for present opportunities in disputed regions undergoing desertification, such as this one. Any fighting over whose laws to apply was convenient. "The problem is the solution." Gray areas made it possible to satisfy a clientele expanding beyond the terminally ill, to include people making rational lifestyle choices.

"I'm going back to the hotel," she said.

Faucheux took a nail clipper out of his pocket. *"Eh oui,* that'll do you good."

But in the end, the men followed Dr. Murchadha along the sandstones covered with scribbles of snail film, and tried not to step on these steady creatures as they marked the pathway to their inner child. On a plant at eye-level went a homeless species without a shell. From this perspective, its slimy body dwarfed a crow flying in the distance. The nine-centimeter slug was ascending a stem leading nowhere. The climber's mucous membrane gleamed in the dew. *You'll be surprised at at the heights I reach...*

"How inspiring, we probably could have it all, if we knew the way to ask," she said. Equipped with both male with female organs, the magnificent hermaphrodite required a two-way exchange of sperm with another slug to proliferate. About the same size as the slug, a heavy Anglo woman padded onto the sea terrace. Four more women passed behind the branches. Suddenly, a troop of young Arab studs spilled out onto the meeting point. Perfume wafted from a jasmine bush flowering behind the ladies. They waited stock-still.

A curious relationship. Dr. Murchadha almost missed the next stepping stone. These unlikely couples had riddled North African resorts for centuries. Sometimes they went so far as to marry, sometimes for more than a visa: for everafter. She had seen a picture of an enormous Welsh bride of sixty contentedly seated next to a youthful stick-figure. The way the old girl basked in her young lover's glory! As if he was the new black.

"These fatties are starving?" the post-doc muttered.

The young Arabs appraised the situation with an air of resignation. It took a degree of professionalism to pull it off, never mentioning the obvious. They let the women make eye contact, then responded to their body language in choosing partners, bantering warmly with the over-ripe ladies, while taking care never to talk to each other. The youths' total lack of machismo was uncanny, despite being witnessed by their peers! A bargain was a bargain. For a month's earnings, the trade was apparently worth it. Even the stud paired with an extremely obese woman didn't show signs of distaste.

Axel looked away in disgust.

Faucheux clapped him on the back. "*Eh bien*, it's nothing, a little survival of the fittest."

Axel rolled his eyes. "The fattest."

"Sure," Dr. Murchadha agreed. "Because our systems haven't totally undermined natural selection, outsourcing our children, incarcerating any advantages evolution might have fitted us with —"

"And animals are better?" the Aussie post-doc said.

"No," she said in a schoolteacher tone. "Animals are much better. They don't destroy their habitat."

It was up to Faucheux to defend the status quo. "Thanks God for death tourists coming at *L'Hôtel Dido. Au contraire*, let them spend their last moments on Earth luxuriating with the natives."

She walked tall.

The post-doc gasconaded at her heels. "What about that beer?"

"Since you set yourself so high above beast, you should have no trouble delaying gratification."

"Ooo," they all guffawed and patted the Aussie on the back. "Another man castrated. Back you go!"

Dr. Murchadha frowned, unsure of her part in

any emasculation, yet positive they weren't evolving in the right direction. It must be hard to be a man.

Axel lit up. "I'm chuffed to bits." A mischievous smile played across his lips. "See, *I* follow the rules."

She gazed at him with an eye used to resolving paradoxes. It was clear. She needed to go back to yearning, with nothing to yearn for.

"At least Dr. Murchadha's got the love thing figured out." Axel was a hopeless flirt. Only kindling burned in that cold heart.

"Now if I can just figure out the work thing."

"The work thing's un-figure-outable," Axel said. "The market is saturated. It doesn't need us or our work."

Sweat beaded on the post-doc's forehead. "Truth! Did you see last week's death toll from opioids?"

Axel stared into a poisonous oleander.

"It may well be the moment for a *petit apéritif*," Faucheux agreed.

"Aye, mate. Com'on Axel, it's on me."

"If money's not a problem, it will be."

The post-doc lengthened his strides. "I can already taste that cold brew."

"All's well in the cosmos," Axel said.

Churlish dimples pierced the post-doc's cheeks. "Axel Harrington, you're an alien."

"Bollocks."

"No, really, my research suggests humans are not from Earth."

The swarm of epidemiologists arrived at Hôtel Dido's back entrance. Squeezing into the glass elevator, she pressed zero and turned around. "You know why there are no aliens on Earth?"

"Why, Dr. Murchadha?" Axel settled his gaze on the tops of their heads.

"They overpopulate their environment before they ever achieve interstellar travel."

Her colleagues tried not to laugh, and looked out the windows. The glass elevator hummed.

Axel watched the sand blowing across the terrace. "Let's just be thankful for glorious Nature abounding." They ascended over two young men coming up the steps. Axel straightened up to his full height and hit his head on the ceiling. "Blimey! Can I get one of those? Makes me never want to date British blokes again. Oh wow, look. He's so dreamy, so sensual, and at the same time, so manly..."

Mercy! She couldn't stand it when he gushed. He could be so porous, outside infiltrating as he leaked into the world. He'd suffocate her. Even if love was just a chemical reaction, she needed some in return. The view of the sea came up. She prayed for another fish. One with Axel's intellect and understanding, a non-smoker, more masculine...

Following Axel's gaze to the sidewalk below the torrid elevator, she scrutinized the well-built worker. He had a goatee. Gold chains glimmered against his white T-shirt. She looked back at Axel, the unattainable, usurping her being. It burned. She felt the suffocating need to get on with her life. She'd even congratulate him on getting his grant, if it meant she didn't have to work with him anymore.

A bead of sweat trickled down her back. She unwrapped the headscarf.

The worker looked up just as Olivia Murchadha's blonde hair came tumbling onto fair shoulders.

She saw him smile.

The Chorus

All existence and energy will continue to recur in self-similar form an infinite number of times across infinite time and space, the waves of Eternal Return.

THE UNAVOIDABLE QUANDARY soon had accents competing at the other end of the table. The chairman raised his gavel and broke up the noise. "Gentlemen. You're probably all wondering why the pharmaceutical industry has invited the insurance, fuel, armaments and other sectors to a meeting of this scale —"

The CEO of an insurance conglomerate puffed his chest. "Who ever heard of such a thing?"

The shuffle subsided.

"Despite our differences, our businesses do have one very important thing in common: they depend on fear. Fear is what keeps people supporting foreign wars, buying oil and insurance and medicating, and fear is what is going to get us out of our current predicament."

The chairman, not a CEO himself, struggled to rally the egos on display around a nouveau-ancient disease no longer trapped in Arctic ice. To get them to wrap their minds around the virus he came at it from different angles, first describing a dormant seed awaiting favorable conditions to sprout, and making the painful mistake of introducing new vocabulary. A 'frozen morphology' reanimated when unfrozen was met with unfortunate wisecracks. Now he was trying to explain, without sounding like a lunatic, how the virus had circulated in the air millions of years before the dawn of man, and guess the reason the modern human immune system had no remembrance of the prehistoric plague.

Luther pushed his microphone aside and raised his voice. "This pandemic simply does not exist."

So the chairman raised *his* voice, "...threatening our leadership if this virus becomes a pandemic."

A chorus of panic seized the floor: *Like that flu in Alaska in 1928? It broke out when researchers extracted the frozen cadaver of a woman from the ice, and she killed 100 million people. Five percent of the world's population. Six times the number killed in World War I.*

Luther looked the board members in the eye. "There really is nothing more deadly than a frigid woman."

The chairman squirmed. A look of helplessness undermined his authority.

Desprez from Sanifree Pharmaceutical struggled to switch on his microphone, "...confusing it with the Spanish flu of 1918."

A Spanish CEO interrupted. "Which did not

originate in Spain. We were blamed because we were neutral in World War One without press censorship."

"It doesn't pay to be neutral," Luther said.

The CEOs shifted in their seats. An Italian aristocrat took off his Solebans. "Let us not waste time." Now global warming had re-evolved a more hopeless scourge. The possibility of even wilder mutations raised the unwelcome spectre of actual devolution.

"A dozen intelligence agencies have turned over every known cell," the chairman stated. "It doesn't appear to be coming from a known terrorist organization, and none has claimed it."

Unless Nature's getting in on the terrorism.

Consensus. They would mount a scientific offensive.

"Gentlemen, let's get down to business. Sanifree Pharmaceutical will present."

Jealous glares fell on the Big Pharma rep. Desprez's wrinkles deepened as he leaned forward again and mouthed a full paragraph before switching on his mic, "...so the hunt for a cure may take too long."

There were a few Mona Lisa smiles. For many, leaving already-afflicted colleagues without a cure would boost their own profits; they just didn't want to catch it themselves.

A suggestion was put forward to fund a

preventative medicine. Desprez halted them with his hand. "There's one already being researched." A situation that pleased many. "An unnamed private individual in Monacco has offered to match our grant."

We know who that is. Board members shuffled through the papers in front of them.

"The funding's for a loveoid. It works like a vaccine," Desprez said, "by changing the body's chemistry to mimic a state of euphoria, much like love. This 'loveoid' sets off an effective immune response that we hope will block the mutation."

"Who's going to develop the loveoid?" a Norweigan asked.

"A team has already conducted advanced research in the field," said Desprez. "Two candidates stand out as potential team leaders."

"This Axel Harrington's qualified, but look at these delays in his deliverables. He takes too long," Shalom said.

An uncalled-for smirk twinged Luther's face. "The woman on the team has a very relevant background. Where's she applied for funding?"

"With us." An American from Biogenetic Vaccines, Inc. retrieved the woman scientist's grant application. He put it up on the screen. It looked precise with reputable sources in footnotes.

A Chinese delegate shook his head. "The man works in more laboratories. He has two times more experience nearly with animal testing."

"But lacks the desired character traits," Luther countered.

"We're not going to bed with them," said the Brit.

A chuckle rippled down the table. Everyone knew the Brits would back Axel. All talked at once. Comments shot across the room.

"Be serious. People need leaders to tell them what to do. We're talking about an incalculable threat. We need a cure, yesterday."

"Don't throw good money after bad. We already threw a two-hundred-thousand-dollar crumb to the Axel guy. It's been three months, and he's gotten exactly nowhere."

"Because it wasn't his idea," said the American.

"Because he's spending our precious time looking for a higher bidder to offer his vaccine to," said the Italian.

"Should we let him know we represent ALL the bidders?" said Desprez.

"Let him figure *something* out." Luther signalled to the chair to wrap it up. "Seriously. We need a loyal worker bee."

"Just give it to the woman. She's programmed to follow instructions. She graduated at the top of her class," said Shalom. "She's a drone."

Hotel pen twirling on thumb, "He's right. We need an overachiever who follows the rules," Luther agreed.

An Argentinian's boney hands crumpled up a memo page. "A meeting gone mad. Come on, the woman?"

"I wouldn't underestimate the woman," the American said. "Her loveoid is backed with solid scientific evidence."

"She could be tougher than the man. Professional women feel they have to compensate," said Shalom. "Nowadays they use artificial insemination and raise their children on their own."

"I'm not sure I trust the woman," said the Brit.

The others reacted: *I'm sure I don't trust the man...ninety-four percent of prison inmates are men.*

Hey, we're gonna need those guys to fight our next war.

Give the woman a chance and she'll outperform him.

Her proposal actually implies a man over forty-five isn't qualified: you have to be able to experience love to understand what to look for in a loveoid.

The men of experience sized each other up: gray slate smeared with the chalk of intrigue and game, where love had been erased. Another chuckle rippled around the table. "Men don't love much."

The chorus prevailed:

It's true. We don't.

I bet women become more loving with age.

Another one of life's little jokes.

"Give it to her. The loveoid was her idea in the first place," said Shalom.

"Peu importe," Desprez said. "All the more reason not to let her develop it."

"She *has* been working on it for years," said the Spaniard.

Luther banged his fist on the table. "Get it done."

The chairman held his gavel suspended in the air. "A show of hands."

A forest of hands sprung from white and gray sleeves.

"Pass."

"The beauty of it is, she's still a woman." Luther was determined to profit from this expensive detour. "She'll be so busy trying to prove herself, it won't occur to her to disobey."

"And if she does, our man Facheux will handle her." Desprez packed his briefcase.

Luther stood over him. "You'll be able to afford that after the loveoid comes out."

Their fate entrusted to the woman, the CEOs rolled out their plan to disseminate the upcoming loveoid amongst themselves.

The New Black

Scientists recently found one-billion-year-old fungi in Canada, changing the way we view evolution and the timing of plants and animals here on Earth.... Previous estimates were that the first land plants existed around 470 million years ago and animals around 580 to 500 million years ago.

— Forbes, May 23, 2019

THE BLAST of cool air calmed the epidemiologists. They stepped into the lobby of Hôtel Dido.

The checkered marble floor was polished to a shine. The wall fountain had been turned off due to the drought, the coins picked over, but the jellyfish chandelier maintained the decorum. A cook in an apron crossed the lobby carrying a bowl with a cloth over it and placed it in a refrigerated counter of cakes too perfect to be good. The bronze wall clock behind the reception showed they were eighteen minutes early for lunch.

A tide of people crowded into the lobby, blocking the scientists' passage. Olivia halted, Axel bumped up against her, and Faucheux against Axel. There they waited while the old people ambled past.

Axel's body stayed pressed against hers. Shackled

to the past, Olivia's heart was dying to deceive itself again. She had to stop forgetting and forget. Throw herself into her work, rewrite her grant application for the ninth time.

Feet planted on a black square, Faucheux lit into Olivia. "Let's focus more on reality, shall we? The sick and dying here in front of us."

"Meaning?"

"Meaning a plain anti-viral would be more practical than your little experiment," he said.

He had a way of driving out the best. "It's not the virus that's harmful," Olivia said.

They all stared at her. She noticed Axel flinch. So the $200,000 funding he'd just received from a UK pharmaceutical was based on the virus premise. Well, that was his problem. He wouldn't be getting a second round of funding without her. She was way ahead of him with her loveoid theory. For Axel, love was a tired game. What a fool she'd been to try to explain it. Some people would never get it.

"*Mais non.* What is it then?" Faucheux demanded over his glasses, eager to hear her theory. "Are you going to tell us?"

Words were trading at such a deep discount; there could only ever be one answer: "Maybe."

"*Eh bien?*"

"Nature has ways of recycling," she said evasively.

"Recycling, and?"

"These scattered fatalities don't fit the mathematics of exponential growth. They're clearly not caused by the virus itself."

"What is it then!"

Olivia looked at her nemesis with a pitying smile. Faucheux only understood symptoms of power. As if she *could* let him in on the Nature of love.

Now that she'd landed in this exile, a mile away from the main facility, to do what headquarters termed 'meaningless work', redundancy was brewing again. She felt it. She had the same bitter taste in her mouth as the last time her job was reshuffled. The machine was in motion. There was nothing she could do to stop it. She exhaled, and cast a pearl. "I don't know, but it's more than the virus."

Faucheux scoffed, *"Genre."*

*

Olivia had to respect these decisive folks padding across the checkered marble, eager for their luxurious going-out party and orientation to the beyond. Those on the lengthening wait lists were more likely to suffer from broken hearts or uncertain futures than one of life's random death sentences. The sick, dispirited and elderly took advantage of this last chance to form meaningful friendships before the transition. Check-in was always heart-wrenching to watch.

A young woman bumped into her. "Oh, sorry. I guess I must be looking forward to this."

Another death tourist turned to Olivia. "You lasses aren't exactly octogenarians."

Olivia smiled.

He rocked on his heels. "They seh t'final act is quite painless, but…"

"It is," Olivia said.

"Oh, I'm sorry, ah don't even know you," the old man said.

"That's OK," the young woman said. "We're in this together." Their freedom to die a voluntary death with dignity had been hard-won. People had been killed defending it. The martyrs who died for your sins. Warriors who met heroic death. Poets. Gurus. The wall was lined with quotes from Jesus, Homer, Rilke, Osho, whose words squarely granted *the fundamental right, for those after living enough and tiring of dragging unnecessarily…to leave the body.*

"Well, it's gran' ta hear what others think about it," the Yorkshire relic said. "I was hoping to find like-minded fowk here. That's what kept me going while ah was making t' arrangements."

"Me too," the middle-aged woman said.

"It's not that ah have a terminal illness or anything, but what with all the drought, food prices are just so high. I'm down to my last 2000 quid. Ah couldn't make up my mind anymore whether it was worth getting art of bed in the morning. I'm tormented by the thought of losing my mental faculties. You know, ah almost missed the bus to the airport weighing t' possibilities, thinking about the physical pain that was going ta come if ah didn't nip on, but doubting that ah really could choose to go my way."

"Of course you can. I spent my last dime on the plane ticket, too. Then I had to stop over in three countries. If I wait any longer, I won't be able to go the way I want to."

"And 'ow's that?"

"In a bubble bath."

"Oh, that's gran'," the old man said.

"With violin music," the woman ventured.

"Oh aye, surely. It's a wee choice," the old man said. "It's our choice, any way we want, they seh."

For a moment Olivia felt almost important. She softened, and broke her own rules, saying to Axel, "You see, it's a meaningful job. This is how it should be. The whole world needs to put more love into their work."

Axel acquiesced in his own brand of passive-aggressive solidarity, "I can't complain about the variety of human specimens."

Olivia's smile froze. And he was her most evolved colleague. How would she ever get what she needed from modern man? A motor was running where his heart should have been. He was completely different when they first met. They must be stuck on some kind of track.

How had love turned to hate? She didn't believe in alchemy. His feelings toward her couldn't have metamorphosed so absolutely. Love and hate had to be two poles of the same phenomenon. She took stock of her polarity with Axel, his eyes stone-cold as if looking at a lobby full of cadavers. You could never pinpoint the moment when love ceased and hate began. Maybe it started with some unspoken doubt. Reconciliation would be a midpoint, where shades of like and dislike were indistinguishable. There was no borderline, just degrees of love/hate, like a thermometer showing degrees of heat or cold or whatever duality the veil pretended to separate, light/dark, East/West. The difference was only a matter of degree.

He still smelled nice.

Euthanasia

Medical reports treat assisted suicide the same as euthanasia, despite its other positions in law.

THOUGH THE JOB wasn't paid as well as working at headquarters, the facility was the best of its kind in the host country. Hôtel Dido had gone above and beyond its remit as the product of a concession in the 2018 United Nations bargain to alleviate overpopulation and bring aid to a climate scorched region. Even if the locals didn't necessarily agree with the cause, many staff members were filled with a sense of purpose, like the waiter proudly jangling his keys while unlocking the door to the bar, and the concierge, who was waving to attract her attention.

She waved back and excused herself. A chance to get out of morning beers with her co-workers. She avoided eye-contact and let the men meander through the lobby in Brownian motion toward the bar for their round before lunch.

Olivia nudged through the crowd.

"Dr. Murchadha!" the concierge said, "How are you?" As a member of the HumanTouch Committee, he made a point of noting hotel residents' moods. She focused on his gold name bar. Latif had her sign a registered mail form and handed over an ordinary looking envelope. The word 'confidential' nagged at her. Olivia braced herself and slid her finger under the flap. The lobby spun. She tilted it away from the concierge.

He said without flinching, "You are fired."

Olivia's fingers tightened around the letter.

"I am kidding. Ha, ha, ha."

She gasped, hands trembling. The HumanTouch committee had gone overboard. She tried to control herself. Stunned, she stared at the letter regarding her grant acceptance. Her heart leapt. Finally! The next line took her breath away.

Latif shot her a quizzical look.

She blinked to be sure of what she was seeing. She got the grant. Yep, there was her name, and the list of her proposed teammates. But this was not just a grant. It was the largest grant she'd ever heard of. She counted the zeros again. A seven billion dollar grant! She'd heard of four billion to bring a medicine to market, but never this much. Was that really the value of her research? Was that the value of anything? ...*funding for tests on animals and humans*. The letterhead was from Biogenetic Vaccines, Inc.

Olivia looked over her shoulder to see if anyone was paying attention to her. Frail tourists fidgeted in line. The trees outside waved in the wind. She was no longer stuck in this familiar pattern, though no one seemed to notice, unless you counted the trees.

She recalled that case where the plants were used as witnesses in a murder trial.

The note paper quivered in her hand: …*to develop a loveoid for treatment of the unloving as a preventative measure in order to penetrate the neural cortex…and enable mankind to escape the fate of pre-Neolithic civilizations…*

Of what? She'd never mentioned research on any ancient civilizations. As far as she knew, there was no such thing as pre-Neolithic civilization. *And why the 'Strictly Confidential' stamped in red on the top of the page?* Her proposal was to derive the loveoid from biochemical processes in the brains of people who died while feeling love. Nothing to do with prehistoric caves. She'd proposed finding a formula using data on slides from biopsies, but the money was for sifting through North African archeological sites! — "Whose idea was that?" escaped her lips.

Latif cleared his throat. "Can I help?"

Outside the lobby, the wind blew swirls of sand around the tree trunks. Subject, object; her, the trees. And still, she had the feeling one more thing was seeing her seeing the trees. The palm tops waved with a conviction suggesting consciousness. Their leaves vibrated so intensely in the wind, they appeared at rest, the fracas ready to tip off the scale of human perception. Sunlight flashed through the leaves.

"Thank you," her lips mouthed. Things were

about to happen for her, she could feel it. She'd never stayed anywhere this long. Five years. The wind subsided. She had the feeling she was no longer alone. A mandala of sun was shining through the palm leaves, casting red, yellow, violet rays in all directions.

She was due for a change. Something had to give. The hope of meaningful work coursed through her veins. As with the spectrum of light and the scale of musical notes, when you reached an extreme, you returned to the next band of colors, or higher octave. If you travelled east around the world, you arrived back at west. If love was simply a higher vibration of hate, where there was love, so was hate. Then she should be able to raise the vibration along the axel of polarization and bring back the love. Nature tended toward the positive...

A black taxi pulled up to the entryway. Waves of heat emanated from the hood.

She felt dizzy. *Seven billion!* A massive grant. Twice the amount she'd asked for. Nobody ever got more, always less. Olivia looked around the lobby to see if anyone was watching. No one was. The letter instructed her to communicate by encrypted email. There was a link and a code comprised of a long string of numbers and letters. She punched them in, and wrote a short note thanking her funders and accepting the grant. She folded the paper and put it in her front pocket. Lips pressed shut, a smile escaped.

"OK. You have received good news. Please accept my congratulations," the concierge said. "Is there anything else I can help you with?" Olivia was about to move out of his range when he added, "How does it feel?"

Feel? Her gaze drifted to the entrance where the porter was waving his hands; there was no convincing the taxi to move out of the way. *It feels a little numb.* This kind of backing was the definition of success in her field, in any field, the Elysian Fields. It would change her relations with the team. Axel would freeze over with envy. She'd have better things to do than dream of his long body stretched beside her like a python sizing up its prey.

Seven minutes till lunch. The others were drinking their beers in the hotel bar. No Axel. He'd shed them like old skin.

By now he must be coiled in the shade with his mouth open...she remembered lying next to him, and the nightmare he had. How she tried tipping him back to love, marveling at his magnificent animal health *for your age,* but her flattery only exacerbated his fear of dying...in the nightmare, he had been sitting beside his own deathbed, consoling his morbid self, clinging to the life inside his healthy self. He'd spent his savings to keep his withered self alive. She watched helplessly as he fretted over how he was going to survive the inevitable. The fear went against everything he'd ever learned. Though he kept his body in tremendous condition, he couldn't shake off this dread, from witnessing overpopulation, extinction. Tossing and turning into a series of symbols, he'd just about invented an entire language, when he awoke stupefied at the good fortune of his continuance. Lying there next to her, Axel stretched his full length...

But she wasn't going to let him charm her into a basketcase. *It feels like hell.* "And you?"

The concierge grinned, teeth clenched, and pointed to a colorful brochure on the reception desk. "Happy. Management wants people to be happy, happy to live, happy to die." He handed her the brochure touting...*a smart system offering customized experiences to connect with guests at every stage of their transition...*

A few old people brambled up to the reception. The concierge handed them brochures. One gasped, turning the page. "Ever arrive in a beachside town and lose all motivation to die?"

"I'll say," her emaciated cohort said. "I wanna go last." Waves of heat radiated from the cars outside the windows with etchings so you didn't walk through. The porter was shouting at the taxi to pull over so a van could get by. The taxi's black windows remained closed.

Olivia's heart beat faster. She flipped through the brochure. Glossy pages offered an array of *mindful* choices: *Massage therapy and cupping. Morphine derivatives and opioids, caring staff, comfortable room with view of the Mediterranean...Final Companions' Escort Service...step-by-step advice on how to savor a realm of new experiences including upgrading to a perfect partner...*leading inevitably to *the transition.*

The two young workers, one thin, with a constellation of acne on his cheeks, the other built with the gold chains, sauntered through the service entrance. Adrenaline pumping, Olivia squinted to get a better look at the one Axel admired. She closed the brochure, hands shaking with jealousy. The title page stared up at her. *How Arab Lovers are Making the World a Better Place.* Unforgettable, especially since the ad would later pop up on her phone. For fear of the many becoming one, she turned the brochure over.

"Chic, is it not?" the concierge asked.

" 'Going into the universal plasma' sounds better than staying alive."

"See? It works!" the concierge said. "We celebrate everything. We celebrate day, and when day ends, we celebrate night!"

*

The two workers stepped out of the service elevator next to the reception. Over the noise, the scrawny worker exclaimed in Arabic, "Look at all these people here for assisted suicide!"

"They're trying to kill us," said the built worker whose goatee almost hid the scar on his neck.

"These old people want to kill us?"

"They want to reduce the Arab population."

"Says who?" the thin worker asked.

"Daesh."

At the mention of ISIL, Olivia avoided eye contact. She dusted off her Arabic. As she eavesdropped, the brochure slipped from her hand. It fluttered onto a black square.

The muscular worker stopped in his tracks. "Oh Allah! The blonde."

Olivia blushed, triggering his fascination. She stole a glance at the worker. His eyes smoldered with sensuality. Her stomach descended to the basement; common sense left her head.

"Laisse tomber, Khalid," the thin worker said. "Don't pick her paper up for her. She's old enough to be your mother."

"What's she doing here?"

"Who cares? She doesn't want you. They're all brainwashed."

Khalid went on staring. *"Elle est belle."*

The thin worker glanced at Olivia and conceded, "OK, she's hot. What's that she's wearing?"

"Business smart."

The thin worker gazed at his friend with the admiration often shown Khalid, not just for his good looks, but because he thought things through. Most people went along with everybody else, but Khalid made up his own mind, and seized opportunities other people missed, even if some were too far-fetched. He was as free as you could be.

*

The clock above the concierge's head said four minutes till lunch. In the mirror, Olivia could see the black taxi outside blocking the driveway. A bus pulled up behind it and started honking. Passengers without a single gray hair descended into the lobby. Youthful guests started to hand in their passports at the reception. "Now I've seen everything," Olivia said.

The concierge leaned closer. "They come through a dating app."

"As in online dating?"

"Yes. Swipe to choose the perfect partner to assist."

"Assist!"

The concierge straightened the brochures. "They're going to be euthanized by a perfect partner."

"Perfect in what respect?"

"In every respect they checked off. Slim, bubbly, soft-spoken, spiritual, whatever they want. We hire them from a local acting school." Latif was looking over her head.

Olivia turned around.

The four doors of the taxi opened at the same time. Two men in black hoods jumped out bearing Kalashnikovs. One punched the van driver. They made for the hotel entrance.

The commotion beyond the revolving door silenced the two workers. *A fight out front.* All heads turned.

The porter tried to stop the aggressors. Folks were backing away from the entrance, when another hooded man hurled the porter through the window. The glass entryway shattered.

People gasped. Everyone froze, gaping in horror as four hooded men in dark uniform charged through the broken window and hauled a bazooka in after them. The hooded men took control of the lobby. Mutually exclusive, they aimed at the flock.

The men yelled their final prayer to Allah.

Olivia screamed.

Where to Find Arab Lovers

Demonstrators took to the streets to protest government inaction, after drought and severe dust storms caused the deaths of more than 1,500,000 people...

KHALID LUNGED. His arms encircled his queen as they fell to the checkered floor, under the spray of bullets.

Those who didn't dive also fell.

A fireball zoomed overhead and exploded behind the reception. The blast sent shards of glass flying everywhere. Everyone who could scream was screaming.

Olivia kept her eyes scrunched shut and clung to the hunk covering her.

Through the smoke, Khalid could see the torso of the concierge, still standing erect at the reception. Unable to peel Olivia off him, he lifted his trophy up with him and looked over the reception counter, Khalid's eyes widened.

Olivia opened her mouth to scream, but nothing came out. She gaped at the concierge's neck, burnt plastic with melted wires sticking out where his head had been. His blue suit jacket was burning. Sparks flared.

"Don't move!" came a disembodied voice, heavy with anger.

Khalid opened Olivia's scratched hand: her room key. Her knees gave way, and he caught her again. Behind thick smoke, he hoisted her onto his shoulder, and made a break for the service elevator, next to the reception desk.

Olivia looked back at the desecrated reception area. Smoke enveloped the headless android.

The thin worker rose from the debris. He shook his head at Khalid, *"Ah bon, c'est comme ça."*

The elevator doors closed. Khalid set Olivia on her feet. Blood soaked through her blouse. They'd both suffered small cuts.

The elevator reached her floor. Olivia's heart pounded harder. Khalid pressed her to the wall as the door slid open. He peeked into the hallway: no one. He ushered her in front of him, down the carpeted runner to her room, plugged the keycard into the slot. The door clicked open: safe.

For the moment.

Khalid wiped his hands on his jeans and scanned the room. He retrieved a cold can from the mini bar and applied it to the bruise on Olivia's elbow.

They listened to the TV in Arabic. A woman newscaster wearing a maroon blazer dramatized the report, heightening the terror as police barricaded the hotel. *Shocking footage shows the full 11 minute ordeal of the attack, leaving at least 39 people, mostly foreigners, dead and 36 injured on a beachfront euthanasia facility...three hundred people taken hostage, no demands.* The anchor said that at least one of the men was a known Daesh sympathizer. *The hotel is in a lockdown. No one can enter, nor exit.*

"What do they want?"

Olivia touched the grant note with the code in her pocket. She had a sinking feeling, what they wanted was her. "I don't know," she said. She watched her savior rummage through the room. He lifted the end of an anatomy book on the dresser, looked underneath and put it back in its place.

"I've got to get out of here." Instead, Olivia sank into the only chair. She kept an eye on his reflection in the mirror.

She had survived against all odds. At least in this universe, where she'd flown like an electron above her body, had existed in the sky and on the cliff at the same time. Perhaps in another parallel, things hadn't gone so well. Maybe she'd lost her cool with her colleagues and missed the railway turntable to safety. And was dead there. The scratches on her hands stung. Blue veins protruded.

Physicists had observed the phenomenon in waves, materializing as particles, that disappeared and then reappeared again somewhere else. Her reflection stared back at her from the mirror. Highly probable in her easy chair, she had a body, and she was a body, usually. But when she wasn't her body, she had many potential bodies. *One mind?*

An hour slipped by peacefully. At least here.

Possibilities must be manifesting elsewhere. To express themselves here, they just needed to play by the laws of this universe. She became acutely aware of the relative lawlessness of her present circumstance, orange and green curtains drawn under siege in their unrecognized territory. *Being the versions of ourselves who survive is only a matter of probability.* She shut her eyes abruptly, thankful to be alive. Afraid to break the magic. The trick was to stay in this universe, while escaping her present predicament. "How am I going to get out of here?"

Treating it as a rhetorical question, Khalid opened the minibar, and fixed himself a whiskey. He sipped his drink while pacing up and down in front of the window and marveling at the sea below. "*C'est beau.* You can see everything from here." He pulled the curtains open wider. "And no one can see you."

"Except the coast guard moored offshore."

Khalid yanked the curtains shut after all, his expression thankful as he turned around and looked at her. She glanced away from his jeans. They were tight. Was he hard? Olivia was not excited by death.

"Muslims don't like euthanasia."

"OK. Why not? They get to kill Westerners. Westerners get to die the way they want, everyone's happy."

He seemed more comfortable hidden. "In our

culture, we have specific ways of killing."

She didn't like where this was going. "And that's why you're against it?"

"It can be used to kill Muslims."

She had heard of that. Population control programs had been used against American Indians. There had been fighting about which population needed saving, which needed reducing, who was overpopulating, who was racist. "These measures have been abused in other countries in the past, but..."

He folded his arms across his broad chest.

Olivia's hands pressed into her thighs. "Look, I have to get out of here."

"You have a plan?"

*

The hours passed.

Olivia wanted to lie down. She stood up instead. "How am I supposed to work?" She should never have come to North Africa. Screw the institute and its useless experiments.

Khalid walked back and forth in front of the window, peeking through the crack in the curtains. "The coast guard's still there."

"We're stuck."

"We?" he said. "So what are you?"

"A scientist. A biologist," she said, trying to sound necessary.

He looked at her blankly. "You have cash?" He reached into her shirt pocket and handed her her phone.

She punched her password in.

He grabbed it back: "No service."

Olivia's eyes drifted to the ceiling. "I always loved animals," she said, unable to keep her childhood memories from escaping as he ransacked her pants. "Animals are free spirits unfettered by human constructs, always ready to play. Ever since I was a child, I was in awe of the unique personalities of each one. Bird, chameleon, feline..."

He looked at her ID card, then at her face, and then read the year of her birth out loud. "You're in good health."

She arranged her hair, realizing he couldn't possibly be interested in her now that he knew how old she was. She put her hand on her hip, accentuating her waist.

"You're American."

"Yes."

He whistled. "A real American woman."

She stopped breathing as he unfolded the grant letter. He sniffed the paper and tossed it on the bed.

"As a girl, I learned everything there was to know about every species."

He came toward her.

Her heart stopped. She looked away, dreading any hint of malice in his eyes, and blabbered on about animals.

Khalid reached into her back, right pocket, then the left. He took out three bills. "We need this," he said, putting the money in his jeans pocket.

"OK." She glanced at the grant note upside down on the bed, the words 'seven billion' printed in black ink. "Then came the horror," she said, trying to distract him. "When I found out that humans were murdering all the animals, I cried for weeks." She looked into his dark eyes. "It was painful to realize what cannibals we are. Because of us, Earth has lost most of its wildlife. All in the past forty years. It just hurt. I spent my twenties circulating petitions to save the whales..."

"You did?" He folded his arms.

"Yeah, and then one day I gave up. After killing everything, humans were killing themselves. It was done. There was no reversing the genocide," Olivia said.

"I like animals, too." His eyes met hers in agreement.

"I wanted to be a biologist because they work with animals." The reality was they tested drugs for humans on animals and killed and dissected animals to keep humans alive longer, all to destroy life on Earth. She'd given up on being a medical doctor. No point in saving lives with no meaning.

"They say Americans are brainwashed."

"Well," remaining agreeable, "they did take

geography out of the American public school curriculum." She remembered the first time she saw a graph of the number of people alive. It was in a private-high-school friend's textbook. The line spiked during the industrial revolution, and then with modern medicine, the population bomb exploded."

"They want to destroy Arabs."

"Nothing of the kind."

He arched his eyebrow at her.

"The fighting's over water and food. The world can't support a population of eight billion. Euthanasia is a solution for people who want to go."

"When people tell me they're going to kill themselves, I want to punch them in the face."

"If they want to go, let them. It's their life. That's what one Indian guru says.

"Who?"

"Osho."

"Humph! That's not what Muhammed says."

"Muh — "

He cut her off. "I don't argue with women."

The TV had exhausted the topic of the lockdown and was decrying the education of former inmates of Camp Bucca, the American prison in southern Iraq now widely agreed to have been crucial in the formation of Iraqi jihadists. *It earned names like 'the Academy' or the 'Jihadi University', where the United States would create the conditions ripe for training a new generation of insurgents....*

"What do they say?"

"The usual: nothing is happening."

"Nothing!"

"To stay in our rooms while they combat the terrorists." He turned off the TV. "One thing's sure. Whatever they say is a lie." He took off his bloody shirt. His chest bare, bronze muscles rippling, a long scar down his neck and the side of one arm.

Olivia tried not to stare at the scar. Gnarled in another attack?

Khalid hummed a snake-charming tune. She listened to him gurgle like an empty water cooler, and wondered if she'd fallen in with an artist. She could almost hear a dinar coin hitting his bottomless cup. Her gaze wandered up to his. "I know you didn't stage that attack to get into my room."

"Ha!" He took a swig of his whiskey. "What sign are you?"

"Whatever's at the end of October."

"Scorpio. *Oh Allah!* Not another Scorpio."

She noticed the scorpion pendant gleaming from one of his gold chains.

Khalid said, "My birthday's the eighth of November."

How curious. Another improbability. She cocked her head and took in his profile with his hooked nose. "Two Scorpios are good," she said, aware her life depended on reaching him on his frequency. "The ideal addition to my hotel room." Maybe he already worked for the escort service.

His eyes lit up coming around to the idea of another Scorpio, the sign of life, death and resurrection, also the sexiest sign of the zodiac. He glared at her over his glass, asking questions to figure out which of the four incarnations of Scorpio he had on his hands, the venomous, possessive Scorpion itself; the slippery, charming snake; the soaring eagle whose piercing gaze sharply observes the landscape and its prey below; or the final ever-burning, all-seeing Phoenix that rises up from the ashes in eternal rebirth... "Not many blondes come in our city. Why are you here?"

"My work as a biologist."

Khalid puffed up his chest. "I studied agricultural sciences at the University of Paris."

"You did! Great. I didn't expect to meet a like-minded soul in this expanding universe of robots." Olivia looked toward the ceiling as if thanking the heavens for a bountiful sequence of events.

He shined with pride. "Are you married, boyfriend?"

"I wouldn't call him either."

"Why?"

"I don't think he can love. He didn't love me, anyway."

"He used you?"

"I don't remember it like that. Maybe he does."

"Do you think he remembers all the chickens he's

eaten? Where is he?"

"I don't know." She choked on the words. *Axel! Was he in the attack?* The orange and green striped curtains hung from heavy wooden rods blocking out the afternoon sun. It didn't feel like he was dead. "He's a colleague. I'm here to work on a…medicine." Making a show of tidying up, Olivia transferred the grant letter to her briefcase, concealed under the desk. "I thought Muslims didn't drink."

Khalid stiffened. "We don't." He emptied his glass and brushing past her, headed for the door.

"Wait," Olivia whispered.

Escape?

Although it is not clear whether there are survivors, police are negotiating with the terrorists for the release of any hostages...

OLIVIA GLANCED at his hard forearms.

"We have a lot in common," he said.

She skirted away. "Like what?"

He met her gaze in the mirror, then went on fluidly, never letting silence mount between them. "I'm also fond of Nature. You should see my farm."

"Where is it?"

"Not far from here."

She remembered Faucheux's words, "The collective neurosis: all Arabs dream of owning a farm, without ever planting a seed."

"You'll have to come visit."

"I don't think so."

"Then I'll have to kidnap you."

The word slapped her in the face. Olivia couldn't believe he actually said 'kidnap'. She let out a little laugh, hoping it was a joke. That was not funny. Did he really want to kidnap her? ISIL would never get her. "I would kill myself first."

"You scare me," he said.

She was waiting to see if he would mention kidnapping again. "A farm…?"

"*Oui, Chérie*, with olive trees, and chickens. Is it OK if I call you '*Chérie*'?"

She could hear the blood pounding in her ears. She looked at him. Was he joking? Suddenly she felt afraid of her rescuer. She had to get out of this hotel. How was she going to find those prehistoric caves?

"It would be nice to have someone cook for me," he offered.

"Ha! That's a new one on me. I like eating cornflakes alone…I suppose room service is out of the question today."

As he talked on about his farm, Nature, how hard it was living on his own, swimming in and out of topics, she was surprised to find his sultry voice soothing. He seemed nice. Did he really say 'kidnap'?

A loud crash shook the building. They hurried to the window. Men were running on the beach, toward the hotel.

Khalid peeked through the peephole, and recoiled.

"What is it?"

He put his hand over her mouth and said, "Look." He guided Olivia's eye to the peephole. She peered into the orange and green hallway: a man pacing up and down with a Kalashnikov. Khalid shook his head, stifling her eruption. "Not yet." He eased his hand off her mouth, and nudged her into the bathroom. Then, he yanked the heavy curtain rod off the window, and dragged it with the striped curtains trailing into the bathroom with them. Olivia noted the mischief in Khalid's eyes, as they prepared to steal back their own lives. He reached out to open the door, and hissed, "Now scream."

"Oh yeah. With my Ph.D. and your muscles we'll just..."

Khalid snarled, "Scream!"

Olivia screamed.

Footsteps hammered down the hallway. Thud, the door shook. Khalid unbolted the lock. Crack, the door burst open. Olivia's wildest nightmare materialized: a man in a black hood tumbled into the room.

Khalid jumped out of the bathroom, elbowed the attacker in the back of the head and caught him under hooded head with the curtain rod, striped curtains streaming like a flag. The attacker's Kalashnikov tumbled to the floor. "Get the gun!"

Olivia grabbed the repulsive piece of machinery and pointed it at the attacker. Khalid tied the half-conscious man up with the curtains. He turned the rod on the diagonal and wedged it into both walls of the entryway.

Olivia's hands felt numb under the weight of the gun. Khalid grabbed it away from her and opened the door. She picked up her briefcase and sidled up to him. "Leave that."

"I can't."

"Leave it, I say."

"I can't go without it."

"Give it to me." He ducked under the strap, neck muscles flexing, and pressed it to his body.

Their feet sank into the padded carpet as they ran down the hallway. Olivia pressed the button for the elevator, leaned against the wall. "You don't really own a farm."

He glared at her.

"Which direction is it in?"

"West."

"Near an archeological site?"

"Yes."

"Near the caves?"

"Yes."

They fell silent listening to the sound of men shouting. Good or bad, fleeing with Khalid was the only idea.

As the elevator approached their floor — five, six, seven — the shouting grew louder and louder. "They're in the elevator!" Olivia lunged for the stairwell. She yanked the door handle next to the elevator and stepped back in horror. A storage room full of androids.

Khalid put his hand over her mouth, stifling another scream, and slammed the door. He dragged her to the door of the stairwell on the other side of the elevator. As he shoved Olivia into the stairwell, they heard the elevator bell sound. The doors clattered open. The arguing brutes.

They scurried down and down again, past the ground floor to the basement. "Where are we going?"

"The service exit." In the garage, Khalid stopped and pulled Olivia behind a pillar. "You wait here."

"Wait? I'm coming with you."

"Wait here, I say!"

"Why?"

His glare silenced her. He disappeared with her briefcase into the bowels of the garage. Her briefcase! Was he coming back? It felt like an hour had passed.

He wasn't coming back...why would a young macho rescue a Westerner?...he probably went off to protect his girlfriend. Olivia's throat contracted. Stereotypes swam through her head, her feet glued to the cement for an infinity.

Beautiful Dysfunction

"Everyone's worried about stopping terrorism. Well, there's really an easy way: Stop participating in it."
— *Noam Chomsky*

FOUR MINUTES LATER, Khalid came back driving a white Renault Kangoo 1.5 dci *camionette utilitaire* with Arabic lettering on the side.

Olivia threw herself into the passenger seat next to her briefcase. So much for her job at the Institute. Khalid gunned the machine out of the garage just as a police officer with an automatic burst out of the stairwell and started firing.

They sped up to the barrier. Practically levitating with fear, Olivia grabbed the dashboard.

Khalid jammed the wheel to the left. "Get down!" he yelled, bullets flying overhead. The mini-truck bounced over a curb and around the barrier.

A police barricade awaited them outside the hotel parking lot. Sirens shrieked. Khalid and Olivia cascaded past the blue flashing lights, and rode on the sidewalk, dispersing a crowd of foreigners who had fled the hotel. Back on the tarmac, Khalid floored it and raced down the street. The Renault engine screeched under the strain.

At the intersection, a woman with a basket on her head stepped into traffic. Khalid slammed on the breaks, covering her in dust and just missing a Peugeot. The traffic locked. They were stuck. One of the cars would have to back up. Khalid rolled the window down and yelled curses at the other cars. "Your god is sucking my —" The Peugeot driver backed out of the way. They skirted through the bottleneck, police sirens wailing behind them.

Khalid pounded on the steering wheel and spit venom at the other drivers. "My dick is big!" Tearing down a market street, Khalid sped up to a bumper, then wrenched the car onto the wrong side of the street and narrowly passed the line of traffic. Three men leapt back up to the curb. "Cult of sissies!"

Olivia raised her head and looked out the rear window. Two police cars were trailing them. "Why are we running from the police?"

"We're running from trouble!" followed by a spew of invectives.

She kept quiet.

At a Renault dealership, they turned the corner. Khalid pulled into the lot, glided down a long line of Renault mini-trucks, and parked in the only empty spot. They slid to the floor. Police lights glimmered on the dashboard.

Seven minutes later, they were on the road again.

Just before the highway, Olivia saw a hotel. "Wait! Stop! I could get a taxi there," still hoping to find the prehistoric caves.

"That hotel has been out of business since the crisis. I'm your protection. We'll go to my farm." He took the first exit. "We'll be safe on the old roads. Don't worry." They zoomed down a narrow route running parallel to the highway.

Olivia was so worried, she was barely sitting in her seat. *How am I going to get out of this?*

The air conditioner was broken, windows down. Olivia gave up brushing her hair out of her eyes and let it whip all around. She watched the desert landscape through wheat-colored strands. Khalid's white teeth flashed through a broad smile. They rolled into the hills. A French radio station was warding off Islamisation with repeats of the 80s song 'Girls Just Wanna Have Fun'.

Their peregrinations continued till they ran out of land. Beyond the escarpment, the turquoise sea gleamed confidently. A black V of birds immigrated from the blue, without permission from anyone. Khalid veered right. Yellow wildflowers graced the rocky slopes and turned the grass a vibrant lime green. The hills trembled in the spring breeze. An occasional olive tree cast a black shadow under the stark sky. Olivia sank into her seat.

Khalid changed the station and sang along to a song with no apparent tune.

The budding countryside stirred a distant memory of sweet lilac that no longer grew back home since they had cemented over the coast, while here, the economy had been at a standstill for decades. "Everything dysfunctional about this place contributes to the beautiful Nature."

Khalid looked at her for a moment, then turned back to the road. "You are a good woman. You are always welcome in my house." He showered her with encouragement, throwing her into relief against a background of shameful people: those who forgot how to take care of Nature, the ones who couldn't manage their own lives, which was the same thing in Khalid's view. Destroying ecology was self-destructing. He liked people who had not lost their connection to Heaven and Earth.

Olivia stared into the landscape. Now the yellow flowers gave way to sand. Low bushes dotted the hills. Tumbleweeds blew across the road. And she was supposed to set up a lab. She looked at the gas tank, almost empty. How was she going to find test tubes out here? "When are we coming back to the city?" The muscles in her throat contracted.

"Whensoever it is safe."

Was he saying that because he wanted to protect her? Olivia caught herself holding her breath. The Moon came up, tilted on its back. Its grimace imprinted itself on her field of vision as they hummed along in the mini-truck with no shock absorbers. "Are there any sea caves in this direction?"

"The best ones in the world."

"Where?"

"Just over there." Khalid pointed.

She looked back at the horizon doubtfully as they passed an exit: too late now. He never slowed down enough for her to jump out.

Two hours of driving through the desert came to an end. They jounced up to a long dirt driveway. Khalid shifted to second. "There's my farm." He pointed at a small whitewashed building on top of the hill.

Olivia stuck her head out the window to get a better look at it. There really was a farm here. The field was striped with green where rows of olive trees grew. A dog ran alongside the fence as they drove up to the house. She heaved a long sigh.

"It hasn't earned anything yet," Khalid confessed, "but the plants and animals are real. More than I can say for Hôtel Dido."

"The android population was out of control there."

"That didn't bother me as much as the people." Khalid thought Hôtel Dido's programmed people were revolutionary. "They weren't human beings anymore."

"They were human doings." Who would have guessed that the first step toward computer consciousness would be humans becoming unconscious? Olivia leaned out the window to smell the hay. One wish come true, fulfilled in an incredibly roundabout way: she was no longer working with Axel. She inhaled deeply. The air was so fresh. She could smell lemons, and he had planted roses. His sensitivity surprised her. "And what were you doing at the euthanasia hotel?"

"Whatsoever they told me."

The only thing androids couldn't do? She dropped it.

He looked straight ahead at his land. "I'm a farmer."

"It must be hard to make a living on a farm in this drought."

He took in her wind-whipped blonde hair. "You can't imagine. Farmers around here are committing suicide. If it rains, there's no one to buy their crops. Five guys were competing to feed my dog when I went off to work in the town. They're virgins. Twenty-seven-year-olds can't find wives. Girls don't want to marry a poor farmer on an arid piece of land. Rich merchants have taken all the women. I'm telling you, fat old men have three families with younger and younger women." He slowed down to crawl around a rut in the long dirt driveway.

Olivia looked at him as if seeing him for the first time.

"It's not much better than Egypt here."

"Is that where you're from?"

"My father is Egyptian. I was born here. But now it's the same thing here. When a fifty-year-old merchant married to his high school sweetheart tires of her and finds a thirty-year-old mistress, there's one less thirty-year-old woman available. If he founds a second family with her, never mind if he marries her — "

"A bit like France."

"France?"

"I mean, they don't marry anymore."

"Then it's for opposite reasons."

Olivia held onto the door handle as they went over a bump. Yes, clearly...if the top third had many wives and the lowest third none... Was there any love anywhere in the equation? Olivia shuddered at the thought of vying for a wife collector. An extreme situation was rolling through the land as resources grew scarce. She looked out the window and wondered where all the displaced young men were.

"We should have stopped at a cash machine. What bank is your account in?"

Olivia stared straight ahead, mumbling, "How am I going to get out of this?"

Before them loomed the un-abandoned farm, the boxy white house, more like a rundown gas station. Khalid stopped the mini-truck under an apricot tree. She stepped into a flock of chickens. Tail wagging, a scraggly dog poked his nose timidly through a barbwire fence.

Khalid yelled, "Wahad!"

The dog cowered.

"Here you have everything!" Khalid exclaimed,

arm sweeping the pink horizon to indicate where everything had been hiding all this time.

She looked at the landscape, 360 degrees of near-desert. Her pockets were empty. He'd taken all her money. She was a woman alone, reliant on her captor.

He reached for her hand so naturally. Surprised, she let him hold it. It wasn't bad to have a friend show her around. They walked into the house together. What was there to be afraid of? Not all stereotypes were true.

In the middle of the courtyard, a bronze cast sundial was ensconced at a southerly angle. The circumference was divided into 12 intervals of 30 degrees, each named after a constellation of stars. The face of Sol in the center was cradled in a slice of Moon. The green rays of oxidized bronze emanated to the twelve zodiac symbols on the periphery. The shadow from a wedge in the middle of the dial was pointing to the sea goat, a mythical animal. As far as science knew. "More astrology."

"You need the planets on a farm. Did you know 'plant' comes from the word 'planet'? Planting and harvesting have to follow the phases of the Moon." He pointed to the fields behind the house. "Otherwise minerals won't absorb, and herbs won't cure." He explained with his hands. Moonlight helped roots and leaves flourish, especially in the first quarter, the best time for planting most crops. His arms drew an arc; Earth was a huge electromagnet, influenced by the gravitational fields of the planets and stars. Lunar gravity pulled water up at the new and full Moon, causing water to swell, causing high tides, causing female fertility, causing seeds to burst, causing lovers to find each other.

If there is water. The clear sky leveled into a darker blue at the horizon. "I bet that clock always works here."

"During the day, almost always. This is the best place for an astrological farm."

A spiritual farmer.

Khalid sorted through a clump of keys chained to his pocket and opened the front door. He took her hand again and led her inside. Olivia had never been in such an empty house. Khalid certainly didn't have to worry about encumbrances.

"Can I go to the bathroom?"

He led her down a dark hallway. "Here."

The window only opened a crack. A rush of rust water splurted into the sink. She stayed there as long as was reasonable, listening for his footsteps. He must be waiting for her beyond the door. She came out and surveyed the living room. A layer of dust blanketed the surfaces. "Can I put my briefcase down here?" she said, indicating one of the two chairs.

"Wherever you want! Make yourself at home,"

Khalid laughed.

Strong arms reached up to part the curtains. Was he trying to make an impression on her? Dark shutters, bolted shut. Khalid went out the front door, then came around outside the window and opened the shutters. They had a view of the vegetable garden. Olivia admired the pink sky on dark green plants, and remarked the expression on Khalid's face, one of primitive gratitude for the gift of life. He had rescued her from danger. He was the one who was going to let her live.

"I've got a very important job to do," she mentioned.

"Superb, *Chérie*. I'm hungry!" He installed her in the kitchen. Then he crossed the courtyard and went into the shed.

Olivia's stomach rumbled. There was nothing in the cupboards, and a jar of butter in the refrigerator. She sat down on the bench. She could hear him across the courtyard and occasionally see his back in the doorway of the shed. Was he working? An ear-piercing screech ensued, followed by a litany of swearing. The noise settled down, just a few footsteps. She opened the refrigerator again. On the bottom shelf was an almost-empty water bottle of green olives. She smelled it — *acrid* — and put it back.

Arms full, Khalid returned awhile later. "Here are some things for dinner." He set his treasures down on the counter, a dead chicken still warm, somewhat plucked "for another day", an onion, two tomatoes, two potatoes, four eggs, a bunch of jasmine, and a dusty bottle of red wine. He lit the stove with a flint lighter and handed her a frying pan. "Let's see how you cook."

"Wonderful!" she said, surprised at how easily he'd taken control. Olivia was flustered in his kitchen at first, but when she realized how few options there were, the task became straightforward, and she ended up enjoying cooking a Spanish omelet for Khalid.

He came up behind her and put his arms around her trying to kiss her neck. She squirmed away.

"*Non?*" he asked, lunging at her again. "*Non?*" he murmured gently.

His embrace was comforting, but... "I don't feel that way."

He slid his hand across his slicked-back hair. "I could have a glass of wine, if you insisted."

Olivia jumped a little realizing he'd already opened the bottle.

He sat across from her in his clean, white T-shirt, bronze arms bulging. Khalid took pride in his body. "And you are American," he pronounced, eyes lit up.

She hadn't seen those stars in a long time. "Well, less and less," almost pleading, "I'm an American in denial."

Then, he leaned back implyingly. "What do you

want?"

She jumped up and filled a jar with the bunch of jasmine. "I don't want anything!" Olivia said.

He gave her a piercing look, raising one eyebrow.

Silence dropped. She stammered, "I don't have any hormones left."

Ha! Khalid's dark grimace said, *We'll see about that.*

"Really," Olivia insisted. "People today don't love much. They're looking for qualifications. It's like they're interviewing candidates for a job. It all depends on what they had before. The perfect catch is a feat of memory. They can't see what life brings them." Olivia sipped her wine. "I'm looking for a man with a long list of faults!"

Khalid laughed.

They stood up. He took the dishes from her hands and set them back down on the table. "Love is a seed." He hugged her gently. His sensuous lips asked, "Why not?"

Pulling away, "You said you had a guest room?"

"In there." His footsteps receded down the hallway. A cupboard door creaked. More swearing. Footsteps returning. She watched him set the sheets down on a chair. Olivia took the sheets to the spare room with nothing but a single mattress on the floor, and closed the door. There was no lock.

Thus began a night of uncertainty. Whether a hostage or just unemployed, Olivia could not sleep. She thought she heard him tap on her door and got ready to refuse him again. At last, the sky began to lighten. Her exhaustion weighed on the crisis, and she fell asleep.

*

At dawn, she could hear the silence ringing in her ears. Her usual state of receivership of news and cultural static had been disrupted. She lay in bed waiting for her own ideas to bubble up.

She hadn't even accepted the grant. The ceiling blurred. A sob erupted, which she quelched. She would go at the first sign of rudeness from him. But he had *already* brought up kidnapping again. How was she going to get back through that desert to the city? What kind of risk was she taking? She was at his mercy.

She tried to open a window: locked. A wave of panic seized her. She tiptoed out into the narrow hallway and walked around the house as he slept. Her body lurched forward, ready to pounce on nothing. She was no nearer to finding the caves or any ancient civilization that might have been resistant to plague. She couldn't just ignore her research. When was he going to wake up? What was he dreaming about? The sheets rustled, then went silent.

A few hours later, she heard him moving in bed again. He must be getting up. The door opened.

Fully clothed, he walked past her. Keys jangled. The front door scraped the cement floor. Now he was whistling outside, opening the shutters.

The panic softened in the morning light. She came into the kitchen.

He set her phone on the table.

A wave of relief engulfed her. She checked that the message about the funding was indeed under encryption and almost smiled. She put the phone in her pocket.

He folded his arms. "They want you."

"I don't know."

"I didn't ask."

Listening to the Air

Desert-FM — we will need two Earths to sustain our collective way of life by the mid-2030s if population and consumption trends continue.

KHALID'S FOOTSTEPS could be heard in the courtyard. She followed him with her eyes as he dragged a water barrel across the gravel. He was a tireless worker on his own farm.

He called her name. It was only to show her which seeds grew what, and explain planting and harvesting by Moon cycle. You had to plant your annual, aboveground fruit and vegetables — corn, tomatoes, zucchini — by the light of the waxing Moon, from the day the Moon was new to the day it was full; and you had to plant flowering bulbs, biennial and perennial flowers, and vegetables that bear crops below ground — onions, carrots, potatoes — during the dark of the waning Moon, from the day after it was full to the day before it was new again.

Every so often, Khalid would go off to spread fertilizer or water his vegetables, then come back and punctuate the peace with his clamorings. Olivia continued to be an enigma for him. He found her drive to research unique among women, never having had one bred for life beyond the family. You knew from the way he hid his surprise behind a blank stare when she spouted some fact about soil density or extinct species.

From the kitchen, she listened to him scraping Wahad's bowl. Olivia let the vegetables soak in the sink. Now Khalid was sweeping off the twelve suns of his signdial. The sun was halfway through the Ram when she came outside. She found a patch of shade and stood in it. "What do you do when it's too hot to farm?"

He seemed to be listening to the air, as if he could tune in to energetic possibilities circulating at higher frequencies. Maybe he could. If you lived out here with nothing, observing potential might be like noticing your elbow. "You meditate?"

He emptied the dust into a barrel. "You may call it that. Otherwise, nothing would work around here."

"You pray."

"If you like."

"You believe in God."

He folded his arms across his broad chest. "As if it's up to *me* to decide whether or not there is God, as you call it. Humph. I am aware of God."

Of course, a North African farmer would be superstitious, no surprise he believed in such things.

He carried on listening to the air.

A physicist at CERN had once showed her an experiment demonstrating such quantum events, where waves at various frequencies collapsed into matter. *Could a frequency cause an experience to happen?* she thought, taking her phone to the bathroom to tune in to her funders.

There was no lock on the door, just a women's clothing catalog next to the toilet. "...I want to thank you again for the grant. No, no, the mission is most certainly not delayed.... Yes, I'm able to work from here." She ran her fingers through her hair. "I'm already ordering the supplies. I just have to know when the money —"

"You have two weeks left before your first deadline. We've sent three mil —" came the loud reply.

She buried the phone in her breast and listened for Khalid. It wouldn't do to be held for ransom. She laughed nervously. "Thanks for the first installment ...I'll be able to finish ordering the materials." That should be worth a few weeks. What she needed to buy was time. She stuffed the phone into her pocket.

*

They harvested peppers in the evenings, since it was after the full Moon, when the sap was high, but the energy had just turned downward. Olivia had to respect their deep red coloring. The peppers had actually done just fine on only partially desalinated water.

Olivia liked to hear Khalid talking to his hens. He strutted across the courtyard and brought back four eggs with the vigor of an Arab man hosting a blonde on his farm. She took in his exquisite hooked nose as he leaned over his cast iron frying pan. He turned each pepper with love. He looked like a real chef. "Cooking is a lost art," she said.

He held up a carrot with two roots coming out of the sides like arms, and made the puppet with green hair dance back and forth. Once it had been peeled, he showed her the knot where one arm had been. An orange eye stared up at her. "See what it's telling us? The eye is a root, to other lifetimes." Through a black lock of hair, his eye rooted in hers. She felt a chill run through to the floor. Khalid mixed his own homemade harissa with olive oil on a plate, broke a circle of unleavened bread, dipped it in and handed it to Olivia. The gesture tranquilized her. She forgot about her trapped feeling for a moment. The bread was good. She loved hot food. They peeled the eggs and dipped them in, too.

She stacked the dishes in the sink.

Khalid was adding bleach to the dishwater.

"Whoa, that's not normal," she said.

"What 'normal'?" His eyebrow arched like a bow ready to strike, his goatee finishing the look.

"Most people don't do that."

"Most people are dumb." He held up the bottle with the swagger of a seasoned pirate.

"OK...I just meant, the average man doesn't wash the dishes with bleach."

"The average man! More robotization, *la!* Turn over all the rocks, and you'll never find your average man. I tell you, not just because of a loophole: the idea is airtight: it leaves no room for reality. The average man weighs 79.8 kilos, has an IQ of 100, and lives in the suburbs of Heaven," Khalid scoffed. "I don't like the average man. If he existed, I would punch him in the face. What you have is a real man."

Khalid was unique alright; he bordered on impossible. "Why change things? We can be open to the world *as it is*. Everyone should be open. Like me." He smiled so naturally. There was not an adjective to describe him.

"Here's the dish soap," she said. "It's better for the environment."

"Fine. I'll use bleach after you leave."

Ah. She stiffened. She was allowed to leave, suddenly wanting to stay.

*

The next evening, Khalid's footsteps could be heard on the gravel as he went to lock the shed. She listened with anticipation for him to come around and bolt the kitchen shutters for the night.

Olivia poured olive oil from Khalid's ceramic jug into a pot, sliced an onion and chopped it into fine squares, taking care to keep her fingers away from the blade of Khalid's enormous knife. She scraped the onion off of the wooden cutting board and into the pot. The hearty aroma of simmering onion filled the room, almost a meal in itself. She grated a carrot and mixed it in with more olive oil, no water. She could hear Khalid humming as she diced three tomatoes and added them to the pot, along with his mother's spice mix. In another pot, she washed the lentils. The memory of one of these stones crunching in her mouth motivated her to sort with care. She picked each pebble out. She boiled the lentils in water alongside the pot of vegetables on a low heat for forty minutes. When both of them were done, she poured the vegetables into the lentils cooked in water and began stirring, her hips swaying slightly with each turn.

This is how Khalid found her when he walked into the kitchen. "Ah, that smells good." He rested his hands on her hips.

Olivia let her 'real man' kiss her neck.

Khalid drew the red curtains. He came and sat on the couch in front of the wooden coffee table. Olivia laid the repast before him and served him first. Leaning over the low table, he scooped up the lentils with his bread. "I get enormous pleasure eating with my hands." He took a bite. "Mmm, where did you learn to cook?"

"A friend's mother."

He took a sip of wine, set down his glass. "I need a wife," he said.

Olivia's back stiffened. The men actually wanted to get married! *Endearing.*

He laughed. "You're still beautiful, my love," he said.

How consoling. Once she'd lost everything to her marvelous young complement, he would go bounding after another gazelle. And yet, he was so different from the limpid companionship she'd known in her North.

After dinner, Khalid took up his lute and plucked a scale of celestial math. The vibrations buzzed to the rhythm of unknown words in a supposed love ballad from Asia Minor, reminding her of nothing. His mood mellowed as he numbed her with unexpected sounds. He was an accomplished lutist. Patterns emerged from hypothetical scales at random, yet miraculously repeated, embracing the in-between. When the last vibration faded, he broke the trance, saying it again, "I'm looking for a wife."

As if there was a sale going on at the market.

He continued, without backing down. "There are many ways to do a family."

"I have my work."

His brow furled with impatience. "Anything for money, even hoping for time to pass faster. When it gets here, you'll be older." He sipped his wine. "You'll never be this young again. Why hurry off?

All we have is now. You have everything, right here."

When they stood up from the coffee table, Khalid extended his arms. Such a warm invitation. Her hands floated up to where they had been when he'd rescued her. She let him hug her for a long time. His cologne carried her thoughts away, as she sank into the protection of his broad shoulders.

"You are a good cook. You'll help me on my farm." His fingers slid down to her waist. "I like a healthy woman, not too thin." His hands felt warm and comforting turning her around. "Come over here." He led her to the couch and sat her in his lap. She fit perfectly into the curve of his body, hugging her torso like a bass, one hand on her stomach, the other on her breast. *"On va faire l'amour."*

Doing Arab Lovers the Right Way

Since 1970, Earth's animal population has declined by sixty percent.

LIFE WAS NEW, like the morning sun on his kitchen tiles while he slept. Just a simple change, and her focus shifted beyond her self-center. An inward smile spread through her at the prospect of this new sacredness. She wasn't the most important one anymore. She tiptoed around, glancing at her poor farmer's body.

Olivia contemplated the last of her mint tea and cast her dawn vision on the world in the cup. A self-sustaining farm was a beautiful idea...but how long could they last on brackish water and moonlight?

She was talking into her Dictaphone when Khalid awoke. He spent forty minutes in the bathroom showering and shaving his goatee. Olivia pressed 'Record'. "Civilization has always meant survival of the meanest. We've witnessed the most ruthless colleagues getting promoted, the greediest getting credit, and in the animal kingdom, the fluffiest, sweetest cats get mauled to death by the feral cats. Developing a loveoid that softens the hearts of predators is a necessary step in steering evolution."

As necessary as the seven billion euros.

Khalid stood in the window. A fierce picture of manly health. His smile overwhelmed her.

If the act of observing could distill a wave into a particle, wouldn't her personality also solidify in the direction of her observer? The day slipped away. Khalid's virility and creativity inspired her acquiescence on chores, ideas, positions. She couldn't decide if he was sentencing or allowing her to feel ways she'd never felt before. A new woman was emerging.

*

Olivia heard pots and pans banging in the kitchen. She opened the door and found Khalid bent over a skillet of fish. A pot of noodles boiled into softness on the back burner. He tasted the sauce, winced and then hammered it with his mother's special spice.

"You only need to cook noodles five minutes."

"Who says?"

"It says on the package, look." She held up the package, all in Arabic, with the number five clearly printed mid-paragraph.

"Because they tell you it has to cook for five minutes, you have to do it? We're people, not robots." He went on cooking the pasta into oblivion. Finally, he turned off the burner, and filled two plates.

Olivia sat down at the coffee table. "Thank you,

Khalid."

His feathers unruffled a little. "Try it."

She took a bite. "Mmmm!" She never in her long life expected to taste something so delicious. The mini-scallops blended perfectly with the pasta and sauce. "Oh! It bites back."

"Really? It's not too hot?"

"No, I can't believe it. I love the pepper. My my! This is the best pasta I've ever had. Mmm." She took another bite, and shook her head savoring the scallops. "How did you do it?"

"Not the way that was written on the package."

"No, really. You have a marvelous talent. I'll have to watch you next time." What luck to have such a voluptuary of Arab cuisine in her life.

"You can't do it."

"Why not?"

"It's magic," he said.

"Then what's the trick."

"I cook with love."

"I can do that."

"I'm a nose. I can smell things you can't."

At first she thought he was joking.

"It's basically chemistry, right? Is that what you studied? What university did you go to again?"

"In Portugal."

Olivia did a double take. She was sure he'd said University of Paris before. In the twilight, the scar covering his neck and torso looked menacing, like a pirate's tattoo.

Khalid flinched under her scrutiny.

"How did you get that scar?"

"Watching my mother cook, when I was four. I was curious about her cooking. I looked into a boiling pot, and it fell on the whole side of my body. I almost died."

She gasped. "Oh no!" It was too horrible. It could really be true, though. He was such a talented cook.

Olivia came back to the table to clear away the last dish, but it remained on the table. Khalid moved so slowly, she didn't realize she was being made love to until she was standing naked, with him pressing into her tummy. His eyes connected with hers in waves as he led her to the bedroom and lay her down beside him. He switched his red lamp on. No hiding. Olivia had never been so confused. The contours of his face smoothed in red, arms strong around her, his beard so cozy, full lips enveloping. She had an inkling mending began with healing their bodies. His kiss quenched such a deep thirst in her. What had been stopping her? She forgot about her inhibitions, and entered the realm of the divine.

"*Changement de programme*," Khalid announced. He laid her back on the couch. "Put your feet up on the windowsill."

This was going to be good.

*

"It's Saturday, time to clean." Khalid handed her a broom.

Olivia raised her eyebrows, not letting her gaze rest on the squalor.

"It's the moment when we're thankful for what we've got." He went around the living room dusting the surfaces while she swept.

OK, she was thankful for the smell of fresh hay in the fields. And the long list of faults she could no longer do without. She was thankful that she wanted a man who was controlling, jealous, one who read the scraps of paper in her pockets. She was thankful that she wanted to scratch with mulberry nails the dark skin of one who quarreled when she didn't clear away his plate. She wanted to pass her hand over the bronze chest of one who, withdrawing, paused, lips touching, poised in an eternity.

At night, he pulled up her skirt and bit her thigh. His other hand encircled her waist.

"How can this be real?" she protested.

"It's natural. The Holy Prophet Muhammad married a woman who was old enough to be his mother."

"No."

"I tell you, at the age of twenty-five, he married the forty-year-old Khadijah. He was married to one woman until the age of fifty…"

"Bless him," Olivia said. She had to love that guy. "A whole country fixated on mother figures.

Incroyable." She'd lucked into a place where wooing older women was part of the cultural identity. She caressed Khalid's back, stoking his passion.

In one swift movement her bra was unhooked and her breast in his palm. She caressed his biceps as he lowered her to the bed. Salvation lay in collapse. He flicked on the light. She was jealous of his lamp shining on the dunes of his stomach, and covered them with her body.

He hugged her closer and whispered in her ear, "Any man who sees your thighs will want to come inside you." He pulled her on top of him. Khalid looked so fresh, so irresistible lying down with dark hair tousled against the pillow. Eyes twinkling. What luck that they had a thing for their mothers. She'd become the matronly figure with whom he could transgress.

And transgress he did.

To have such a young lover who seemed so taken with her. How could this be? "That's it," Olivia said, drawing away from her magnificent man. "I'm crazy. You're not there."

His eyes gleamed.

"You're impossible," she ranted, brushing his lips. How could he be real? The mix of asceticism and sensuality was sucking her into hysteria. She never would have dreamed this arid land could produce such a gifted lover.

Carefully laid on her body, her cactus flower

confessed to her, "Making love with you is *énorme*. I've never been with a woman like you. I've never made love like this, and I think I never will again." He kissed her, his exotic mother, one of his choice.

Olivia ran her nails lightly over Khalid's back. He did seem in love. Was it his Oedipal complex talking? *You probably say that to all the women.*

He rested his chin on his fist. "How important is sex to you?"

"Very." She had quite forgotten about her work.

"Yes. It's creation. That's why the god Aramazd needed his wife Anahita."

"Who?"

"An-a-hi-ta, the goddess of fertility, wife of Ar-a-mazd in ancient Persia. Like Osiris and Isis, Shiva and Shakti, the Greek ones, who were they?"

"Zeus and Hera."

Before monotheism, the divine was couples. "It's in everything. '*Le plafond*' is masculine. '*La chaise*' is feminine."

At that moment, gender really did seem to underlie everything. She'd heard theories on the formation of crystals resulting from sex activity. "All this time I thought chairs were masculine."

"That's Italian...who cares about the f— chair."

"And how important is sex to you?" She caressed his hips.

"Good question. I don't know. Right now, very important."

She listened to his soft orders, assuming the desired position, to attach in the most pleasurable connection, and relinquish license to cause so much pain, once life inevitably separated them. As he withdrew, she followed him with her hips, detaining him inside her. The last stillness sank into the sheets.

Khalid faced her, eyes still penetrating.

Olivia sighed. "You are..." She searched for the word, "deep."

"?"

"One can dive and dive."

"Then dive."

*

At noon in the bathtub, he kissed her ankle, and hugged it between his ear and shoulder. The bubbles popped. Rubbing the knotted skin that covered his neck, he got out of the bath. "Should I tattoo over this scar?"

The scar wasn't pretty, but it was manly. "No!" Could it really be from a childhood accident? Goosebumps appeared on her arms and legs. Either way, tattooing over the knots in his skin would be a cop out. A loss of the masculinity that she was becoming addicted to. She stood up in the bathtub and wrapped a towel around her hair like a headscarf. "You want to hide the tattoo that Allah gave you!"

He bowed his head. "That's good."

The Hunt

WNYF-FM — Damages from Hurricane Deja have brought eight-foot floods to New York

THE DRIVER TURNED off the car radio. "We're here, Sir."

Heavy clouds jettisoned sheets of acid rain onto the skyscrapers. Microparticles of diesel soot slid down walls of glass to the ground floor. They seeped into a network of pipes running underground below minus five and into the gray waters of the Hudson.

The guard kept his eye on the TV monitors. Static filled the screen as he switched to a view of the Millenium entrance with the revolving door where two of the top twenty CEOs were accessing the building. Two board members were escorted past giant pots of gardenias.

The businessmen came through the revolving doors in front of a delivery man bundled in bulky winter attire.

The doorman stiffened. "Sir, please take off your raincoat and put it on the conveyor belt before stepping through the metal detector."

Rather than unzipping his raincoat, the delivery man started arguing with the doorman.

The guard at the TV monitor spoke into a microphone. "Let's go!"

Another two guards appeared inside the door. One yanked the CEOs through the entrance and barred the door. Before the delivery man could reach under his coat, three policemen ran up the steps.

The delivery man whirled around to face the policemen, with their guns aimed at the delivery man's head. He man raised his hands.

The CEOs were hurried into the elevator. At close quarters, a strange bump became noticeable on the shoulder of the last one in. The other two averted their eyes, hoping it was just a gun sling.

"Where is that woman scientist?" one said.

"Apparently in an area without 5G," said the other. "We haven't been able to lock onto her coordinates."

"I thought 5G was everywhere."

"So are sandstorms."

Why Arab Lovers are Impossible

This is Desert-FM coming over the waves. Three leading universities have closed down their Muslim prayer rooms...

SUCH A RARE SPECIMEN, she thought, standing in front of Khalid. He really did love her, right now. Sorrow engulfed Olivia. She melted into his arms. "I'm crazy in love with you. I love your hands and your lips and your arms, your nose." She caught her breath. *What am I saying?*

"I love your ass. *Caresse-toi, Bébé. Je te baise.*" He picked up her hand and ran her fingernails along his inner thigh. "*Suce-moi, Bébé.*"

While she looked into those sensuous eyes, her hand opened his zipper, and slid down to his cock, well-formed and comely.

"And you're blonde," Khalid said, "and you're sucking me." His olive lips said, "You and I are never going to separate."

She straddled his hips.

"If you were my wife..."

"If I were Muslim, if you were older," if, if, if, masking and unmasking this impossible love.... "And you want to get married! Isn't it better to remain in love as long as possible than to kill it with marriage?"

"No."

It was dark outside. Khalid fell asleep. As he slumbered on, doubt gnawed at Olivia. It was too much, too fast. It couldn't be real. Not wanting to be seen with her, then talking about marriage. This was so crazy...what was she doing here? The farm was a long way from anything, even a house. Olivia could scream if she wanted, and no one would hear.

She tossed and turned that night, dreaming intermittently about a relationship that started off as a borderline case of kidnapping. If Khalid knew about her backers, he would certainly hold her for ransom. In addition to not fitting the role he'd picked out for her, she couldn't sleep until noon. She gave up at five thirty a.m. This was crazy. She was about to lose everything. Where were the keys? She got up and paced around peeking in corners. Then, she stood frozen in the middle of the living room. He'd left the house unlocked.

Was she free to leave? This would be the moment to escape. The countryside breathed in the purple pre-dawn. She knew what she had to do.

She grabbed her pants from the chair.

"Where are you going?" Khalid asked, one eye open.

He's awake. Khalid's intuition was on target.

"If someone doesn't want to be with me, I don't

run after them, " he growled. "I'm a man."

Maybe he did really love her. If she left, he might never take her back.

*

That evening, Olivia stood in the doorway, a silhouette, saying the inevitable. "Don't you ever want to go out?"

"No."

"You don't want to be seen with me?"

"I told you."

"No you didn't."

"It's for professional reasons."

"I know there's an age difference, but most of the men I've been with have been proud of me. They wanted to show me off. Are we hiding from someone? I mean, I still turn heads."

"Turn heads!" Khalid recoiled. "We have to worry about you looking at men in the street!"

"We can't even get out of the truck at the same time. I didn't want to bring it up, but it's spooky. How can this ever work?"

She followed Khalid out to sprinkle the chicken feed. He reached into a pot and dropped the seeds. Then, "I was invited to a party."

Olivia's heart leapt. She followed him into the house. "Would I have to cover?" She'd seen the pictures of the women in his family all in headscarves.

"No. Why? Don't you want to show that you're with me?" He was combing his hair.

"It's not that. I just think we should honor our bodies."

"You think your religion is better than mine."

"The West doesn't honor the body either." Making students sit in classrooms for years, molding them for sit-down jobs. Farmers had the edge when it came to moving your body. "The body is the key to mental health."

"It houses the spirit," he agreed.

She stroked his chest. "Just like the planet houses the human race. No wonder humans degrade the environment."

This line of reasoning appealed to his Scorpio sense. "We'll go out!" he announced.

"Oh! Well, great...could we go to a restaurant in the city?"

"No. We'll go to the barbecue. Wear whatever you want. I'm wearing this."

She scanned his jeans and polo shirt, and decided she would bring her hijab just in case.

Outlandish

Government troops blew up the levy and flooded small farmers' land. Three weeks later when letters were sent to each offering to buy the land, the farmers resisted. Their freeway exit was shut down, the tarmac taken from their road, leaving it as gravel.

OLIVIA FINISHED showering in minutes and threw on her clothes. She paced around the farm while Khalid shaved. The pine sap melting in the sunset smelled like freedom.

Riding past the fields with the windows rolled down, she felt so well under twilight's caress. The last of the sunset faded into the black of night. Khalid switched on the high beams.

The drive was turning out to be long and bumpy. They'd been on dirt roads for a half an hour. Couldn't he find the way? Her hand clenched the car door. She regretted insisting they go out.

When he finally found the freeway entrance, there were no street lights. Olivia fidgeted in the passenger seat as they meandered farther into the pitch. Khalid had to drive at a snail's pace.

Two hours later, they arrived at a street packed with double-parked cars. They passed an enormous villa. They'd have to walk back. She prayed this was not a trick. As she stepped onto the pavement, voices and laughter wafted out of the garden.

Olivia's muscles relaxed. There really was a party going on. Now to find someone who could drive her back to civilization. "Whose house is this?" she ventured.

"The mayor's."

The mayor! Olivia kicked herself for doubting Khalid. "You know the mayor?"

"Everyone knows him."

"Everyone knows him?"

"Oui. He was born and bred in France. His family moved here when I was fourteen. He went to my high school." Khalid said, sniffing the air. When they reached the side of the main house, he bent down to look at the mayor's vegetable patch. "Let's see. What's that, *usufruit?"* Curious about what kind of fertilizer the mayor had, Khalid bent down and sniffed the dirt. He peeled a garlic clove and bit into the meat. "A very healthy plant!"

An overgrown thicket separated the house from the back garden. As they walked through the hedge, a man stepped out of the shadows. Khalid whirled around to face the silhouette.

Olivia almost peed.

"Khalid," the man called.

"Jean-Pierre!" Khalid said, surprised to see his oversized friend. They were all like that in the mayor's clan. Large-boned bourgeoises with an overabundance of flesh.

"My hermit friend, to what do I owe this rare visitation?" The proud mayor extended his arms in a florid welcome, then pulled away. "Allah, you stink!"

Khalid chucked the rest of the garlic into the bushes. "My land gets dryer every year…"

"Keep coming around here and I might have to grant the permit for your well."

"If you can put aside your own interests for a minute."

The mayor chuckled, wrapping his chubby arm around Khalid's shoulders, then enmeshed Khalid in a tangle of verbiage as he led them deeper into the hedges.

Olivia couldn't pinpoint what was strange about their host. Although his walk was more like a waddle, the mayor's comportment was that of a real Frenchman. She skipped closer to get a look, but the path through the bushes was too dark. Emerging from the thicket, she caught sight of a filament dangling from his elbow. They came out into a clearing where a black Renault coupe was parked in the grass with the keys in the ignition. A cluster of guests in Western dress had gathered around a table on the verandah. A teenager in a shimmering top went by with a red smoothie. "The mayor's wife," Khalid said.

Then, a heavyset woman, the mayor's senior wife, held out a tray of assorted juices. There was no alcohol. Khalid greeted a few guests, but when he opened his mouth, they shrank back from his garlic breath. One turned around and whispered, *"Le paysan!"*

Khalid was the least practiced in small talk, and openly bored by this urbane society. Isolation descended around Olivia. Her headscarf was too warm for the humid spring night. She unwound the hijab, revealing her unthinkable hair. Heads turned. A low growl emanated from Khalid. By now the wife was introducing Olivia around. Olivia missed most of the names, except for Mosfiloti. She wondered whether he was too old to drive.

"Olivia?" cried a woman with tattooed hands. "I had a bitch named Olivia! No offense, but that dog pooped all over the house. She ruined my Persian carpet. We finally had to change her name."

"The mayor's mistress," Khalid whispered.

Lips frozen in a smile, Olivia wondered if the woman had a car.

A breeze carried over the smell of burning fat. The mayor's brother was barbecuing choice cuts of meat, which Khalid flatly rejected, suspecting it might not be halal.

"Never mind," the brother said. "I'll bring out the fire water!"

The mayor sneered at his brother. "You think you

own the place."

"Who's been doing all the work around here since you started turning? You ought to move from the couch more often." The brother mumbled, engrossed in a kebab.

"I move just fine!" The mayor shouted with machismo, surveying all that he owned, and his blasé guests, too.

"Only to wander off to be with the bushes."

"I'll show all of you...." The host raised his voice so everyone had to pay attention. Khalid and Oilvia tried to listen amiably, but it was annoying. He ensnared you in a noose of verbiage so tight, you couldn't think your own thoughts. If he ran out of things to say momentarily, he'd sing a few bars of a song to prime the pump until the supply of words was replenished, detailing everything that had happened to him, everyone he met, as if you didn't have a life. He accused the guests of underestimating their own proportions. "Man is a tree with his roots in matter and his branches in..."

"...in a *potage magnetique*.... I know." The brother's eyes narrowed against the mayor's oral inundation.

In the floodlight, Olivia noticed the green cast to the mayor's face. She edged closer to get a look at the strange filament poking out of his arm. An aerial root! Her eyes locked with Khalid's. No one else seemed bothered by the mayor's orchid-like tendril reaching out to point at nothing. Olivia scrutinized the chloroplast cast to his skin and tried to fathom what kind of disturbance could have caused such a need for grounding that he sprouted a root.

"An energy cord," Khalid whispered.

"A what?"

Khalid insisted: if you focused on it, you would cord it. Olivia considered the existence of energy structures that extended out of you to connect to other energy bodies, people, places, animals, or objects, when you interacted with or thought or talked about a person.

The virus resided in the solar plexus. If it triggered the mayor's DNA, the mutation would probably start there as well. Looking at his lumpy shirt, Olivia had a hunch that the mayor had sprouted more cords from this area.

"See that?" said Khalid. It turned out the solar plexus was also the main seat of energy cords. Once the probe connected, energetic information would be transmitted back and forth, to and from the target. "Sometimes people can steal your energy," Khalid said.

The brother filled the empty glasses, and turned to their guests, who were passing around a curious artifact. "We found it together, so technically it's both of ours."

"I found it," the mayor said.

"Where?" asked Mosfiloti, examining the object fossilized in amber.

"Near the caves."

The next person held it up to the light. "Did you find it when you started drilling, or at the bottom?"

"All the way at the bottom of the well, around 30 meters down," said the brother.

The mayor started to shake. "Put it back on the table." His root bobbed, absorbing humidity at eye-level.

A man with a black and white *keffiyeh* set the relic on the table. Now Olivia could make out the enormous, humanoid-looking front tooth buried in the amber. Her hand seemed to reach for the fossil in slow motion. If only Faucheux could see that! How jealous he would be, even if he'd never be able to see through his indoctrination to understand it. The creature must have been three times the size of modern man. Most of the known titan creatures predated man. Mammoth elephants, the giant kangaroo, which died out earlier than 50,000 years ago. This would put it *any time before that*. She'd never seen anything like it; this would be the only known fossil of its kind. The tribe at the sea caves must have lived longer than the rest of their species. Perhaps their humanoid civilization was exposed to the same mutations people were experiencing now.

She was so glad she'd come to the party. Olivia turned the petrified molar to get a look at the other side. What a breakthrough that would be, to find out what had enabled their survival. Fascinated by the solid amber, she had to find the key.

The mayor dropped his plate of lamb, peppers, chick peas, potatoes and carrots in the grass. He waddled over to the table. The mayor issued a wave of floridity ending with, "...the relic's going back where I found it." In a zoetic shiver, his green tendril wrapped around Olivia's wrist.

"Don't touch my woman," Khalid snarled. He sized up the root from different angles.

The guests pretended not to notice.

Olivia contained her horror, finally able to examine the mutation in its early stages close-range. The root was much more supple than she'd imagined. She checked his torso for any diverticulitis of the intestines that might be sprouting into roots. His lack of empathy as he spoke with disregard for those trapped listening, suddenly gave way to speech atrophy. "But that relic is a wonderful find," she probed. "Look at that amber. It might date from an era before Homo erectus lived on this terrain." She looked into his blank stare, *Could the mayor still reason?* Then she tried, "There are rules about the ownership of archeological discoveries."

"R- r- rules ch- change," Jean-Pierre growled through clenched teeth. His face turned a darker green. He struggled, but was unable to say more.

Olivia's eyes met those of the teen wife, who averted her gaze in defense: her husband was still a man. Olivia figured the mayor only had a few hours left before he joined the hedges. He didn't seem like the type to transition smoothly.

The brother forced his way between the mayor and Khalid, offering them a plate of kebabs. The mayor scooped a few of these up only to drop them on the ground, his tendril still fastened around Olivia's wrist.

Everybody watched Khalid bounce-stepping. The brother tried to change the subject in the hopes of getting the mayor excited about the upcoming election. "That's why it's important to vote. See, you don't vote for the guy you like. You vote against the guy you hate."

"When you vote, you vote against yourself." Khalid fixated on the mayor's root wrapped so tightly around Olivia's wrist, the blood had run out of the vine, and it drained to an eerie white.

"You have to vote, to stop stupidities," the brother said.

"Like euthanasia," the mayor said.

"I'm interested in that." Mosfiloti's silvery hair shone in the floodlight.

"In what?" Khalid's nostrils flared.

"What you just said."

A look of incredulity spread across Khalid's face. "*Euthanasie?*"

"*Oui —*"

"They're trying to kill us all," Khalid scoffed. "They did it in the thirties."

"— I want a soft death, before I become dependent on everyone around me."

"You're the exception, then," Khalid said.

Mosfiloti sipped his wine. "I'd rather make my own arrangements comfortably and leave a small footprint."

The brother raised his hand. "You'll have another good night's sleep in our guest room, and you'll feel better in the morning."

"No one would willingly die," Khalid sneered. "No one."

Several guests agreed with both Khalid and the mayor. Euthanasia was wrong, but they would rather take matters into their own hands when the time came.

"Humph." Khalid was shocked. "People who want to die!" He leaned into the mayor's appendage wrapped around Olivia's wrist. "My parents had six children so four could live." Spit sprayed from Khalid's mouth onto the mayor's cheek.

Mosfiloti smacked his lips, pretending not to notice Olivia's arm under siege. "Khalid, you listen to the news," the old man said in a calming voice. "The world is overpopulated. Young people are looking for meaning, but there is none. There's certainly no meaningful work. All we do is pollute the ecosystem. Once your juices dry up, what else is there to do but merge with Nature?"

"Excuse me, but Sunnis will never tolerate that,"

Khalid snarled.

"In any event, voting is *essentiel*," the brother said, moving in between Khalid and the mayor. "Obviously, violence is not the way to solve things."

Eyes dropped to the floral tablecloth, but Khalid was too wound up. "It is if you push it."

The brother eyed Khalid's muscles. "That's so cliché."

The mayor grumbled, his root pressing further into Olivia's wrist as she tried to unwrangle it.

"Sometimes you have to use force." Khalid nudged the brother's shoulder. The brother back stepped into the mayor.

Olivia shrank back, her arm stretched to the limit.

About to snap, the tendril released Olivia's arm. The mayor and his brother both staggered away from Khalid.

Olivia immediately stepped into a group of women and said in a low tone, "Maybe one of you could give me a ride."

"Where are you going?" the woman with the tattooed hands asked. She pointed her car out, the Renault saloon parked behind them in the grass. "Yes, there's a hotel you can stay in. You can take the bus in the morning."

Olivia hugged her. The brother refilled their glasses. The party was laughing and joking again. The Moon hung on its back in the sky. A cool breeze chased away the mosquitos.

Presently, the *Varrroom!* of a motor drowned out the conversation. The bright lights of the black Renault saloon blinded everyone at the table. The guests suddenly realized that they were staring through the high beams at their host in the drivers' seat. He spun the wheels into drive. The car was coming at them.

Paralyzed in disbelief, they remained in their seats, waiting for a sign.

"Attention!" Khalid yelled, startling the guests.

The woman with the tattooed hands screamed, "My car!"

The guests dove to either side, just as the mayor drove the vehicle over the lawn chairs and into the barbecue. A heavy woman who couldn't move fast enough thudded against the hood. Her body went billowing into a bush with the merguez, a spicy Ojja stew of lamb, olive oil, garlic, peppers, tomatoes, harissa and egg, and a fruit salad. Bottles shattered. The Renault sent a cooler full of ice and beer flying into the veranda window, and the amber relic into a deco pot at the edge of the terrace. The car mowed down the last table, then crashed into the house. The hood popped open, engine steaming.

But the mayor was still able to back up. He tried to maneuver in his brother's direction, running over a tiramisu. "S- s- see if I can't move — ha!"

Olivia lifted herself from the disaster and sidled over to the terracotta pot. She reached in and grabbed the fossilized tooth.

The brother waved his arms, *"Au secours!"*

With unexpected agility, Khalid sprang toward the car. He wrenched the driver's side door open and yanked the mayor out. The mayor toddled on his feet, but didn't fall down. Instead, his tendril extended and wrapped around Khalid's neck.

The guests gasped as Khalid pulled the tightening root off only to have it wrap around his arm.

Sweat pouring down his jowls, the mayor swung. Khalid ducked. Though the mayor attacked several times, Khalid dodged, and to everyone's supreme satisfaction, threw a punch that gave the mayor a big, fat, black eye. 'Garlic-Breath's' popularity skyrocketed.

The show ended with an elbow to the mayor's gut, whereat his obese body doubled over. Khalid swiftly raised his fists and cracked the mayor on the neck. As the mayor thudded to the dirt, his aerial root stretched to its limit and snapped in two.

Olivia pulled a piece of cellophane off a fruit salad on the lawn and collected the aerial root. After sealing off the sample, she wrapped her hijab around it.

The guests stared in astonishment at the scene they would still be dreaming about in their beds that night: Khalid opened the trunk and hoisted their massive attacker off the ground. The mayor's head lolled. "I- I- I'll never approve your well!" he sputtered, with dirt on his nose. "I spit on puny farms!" Then, he managed in one last effusion, "They're a hazard. The ss- su- supply and distribution of food will be restricted. I revoke your w- wa- water rations, your farm can —!" A gurgling cry ripped through the night midway between the Nile and the Atlantic as Khalid stuffed the mutant into the trunk and slammed it shut.

No one moved.

Unprofitable Oil

Governments worldwide subsidize the fossil fuel industry to the tune of $5.3 trillion dollars ($5,300,000,000,000) a year, a gross misallocation of the amount spent worldwide on public health.

DIALING THROUGH the static, Olivia found Khalid's favorite music station.

Khalid swerved the car onto the highway. "There! We went out."

"It was —"

"Don't start," he boomed over the radio. "It's dangerous to fight in the car."

"I'm not fighting."

Khalid held up his finger. He'd had enough of her saturnalia; he was tired of Sunnis; he was his own God.

Olivia clutched the relic and the mayor's aerial root, hidden in her hijab and kept silent the rest of the way home.

Back at the farm, Olivia marched through the courtyard.

Khalid cavilled about her *manière*. "Still turn heads," he said in a gruff tone. "Paying to die!" He slammed the door and locked them in. "Bring me a beer."

Olivia slunk off to the kitchen. She hid the relic at the bottom of the clothes basket and came back with two Celtias. When she couldn't stand smiling and nodding anymore, she pretended to be absorbed in folding the clothes.

Khalid rambled on about what he might do to a figurative woman. Whenever he talked about another woman, obviously he meant Olivia: "If I ask a woman to be my wife, and she wants a marriage contract with all her money, and still wants me to participate in paying for things, and drags me out to restaurants to eat in a private room upstairs, I might throw her out the window! I don't want *filet mignon*. I want a hard-cooked egg *à la maison*."

It was like that story about the teenager who turned into a cockroach, but with a woman who turned into a dust pan. He finally settled down on the couch with his lute and plucked a series of atonal love ballads of diminishing tenderness. Once he had assimilated events into a steady rhythm, Khalid played a final future-perfect complaint, then stashed his lute on the shelf.

Out of the corner of her eye, Olivia watched him go into the bathroom, keys dangling from his belt loop. He came out a few minutes later naked, without the keys.

So that's where he hides them —

He snatched her up. "The honeymoon is over.

Now you are my slave."

She recoiled. "As if I studied my whole life to just give it up." Her knowledge. Her convictions. *And then love him for his naughtiness, too.*

It wasn't enough to possess her body. He wanted to know that she sacrificed for him. "I've never been so nice to a woman. I'm tired."

He seemed wide-awake.

Your Wife

Rising temperatures have created a pool of more than 100 million people in mass migration, numbers not seen since World War II. Farmers have been driven to despair. Some have committed suicide, others have left their land.

DRIFTERS TRAIPSED onto the farm. Half a bushel of apples disappeared. A tub of cheese went missing. They'd seen one haunted vagabond eating dirt along the roadside.

Discussing osmosis, mineral transport, and how the link between human and plant seemed closer than they'd suspected, they were surprised by another drifter, who had the nerve to trespass during the day. Khalid growled, swore and threatened, but the emaciated man went on pleading and walking toward them. Khalid grabbed his scythe and chased the tramp off the land.

Farming dry terrain had taught Khalid a great deal about Nature, human and otherwise. That night, he kept a lookout through the cracks in his bolted shutters.

The wind blew dust into the air. The water level in the river lowered to alarming levels, increasing toxification and its bizarre side effects. Villagers were at risk for all manner of illness, according to the news, although the area must still be cleaner than the West, where the drop in sperm count was over fifty-two percent.

*

A look of helplessness flashed across Khalid's face. He noticed Olivia watching him, and conquered the emotion. "We need to find some rabbits."

"Rabbits!"

"Eh oui."

"Not to eat."

"To breed."

"To sell to...butchers?"

"If anyone wants to buy them," Khalid said.

"I thought you were just going to sell crops and eggs."

He arched his brow. Forearms tightened, his muscles no longer inviting, "At least we let them live in the first place."

"But we don't need to kill bunny rabbits!"

He carelessly said the words she'd keep hearing over and over. "I see why your colleague didn't love you." The lightning bolt shot through her. It was meant to hurt, even though she knew the truth. Axel didn't love anyone. The only thing he could understand was his little game. The mistake was exposing her weaknesses. She took her wounded pride into the kitchen before the tears came.

Khalid followed her. "Stop walking away!"

This relationship demanded qualifications she didn't have. She could never foresee his sudden precipices. Few men had ever tried to control her; none had succeeded; and she had never wanted one to.

"You're too independent."

She opened her mouth and shut it again. Then, "Of course, I'm independent!" The tears were streaming now. "I've worked hard for it. That's why people go to school and compete for jobs. Something you know nothing about."

She had shut Khalid up. Victory.

He looked cowed and went all passive that night in bed.

What to do?

He lay on his back in uncertainty. His eyes drifted to the ceiling while she took the reins.

"What happened?" she asked, but he just looked up at her, forlorn. She caressed his chest. Best not to do anything that might hinder his performance. That night, she discovered her quiet power. "Maybe that's where Western society went wrong…"

"There are 360 degrees to every circle."

"It would be much easier to end this now than trying to make me into your wife," she said.

"As if we had the choice…" he hissed, a serpent of

words swallowed in ancient Arabic.

Abjection strengthened his magnetism. Now she thought she could feel the voltage between them, filaments reaching, connecting...of course energy was the epiphenomenon of matter. Olivia stretched, blood circulating, life force reactivated, "Forget what I said. I take it back."

Too late.

The next evening, instead of following her into the bedroom, he left her alone.

Olivia let it roll through her. Never mind. He would come when he was ready. She sat behind the house with the stray cats. The locals never let these indigenous beasts into their houses. Khalid had taken care of one family from birth when they crawled out of a bush meowing, eyes sealed shut with conjunctivitis. Now they were fine, just a little teary, and more tame than most.

The sun set into a tin-colored twilight over the fields. Little bats celebrated, swooping through the garden. One fluffy, feral kitten saluted Olivia with an all-encompassing meow, and lay beside her on the steps. She stroked its black fur into a frenzy. The baby creature was so appreciative of the attention, Olivia couldn't help herself. She'd wash her hands afterward. She scratched his cheeks, his back. He rolled over, *pretty kitty*, and she patted him on the tummy.

The Earth would eclipse the Moon in forty

minutes, an astronomical event. Strange, little, white cloud puffs floated across the horizon. The Moon's full, crater-etched face peeked through the fig leaves. The kittens jumped in and out of a terracotta urn.

It seemed within the orange supermoon lay the memory of Khalid prone on the bed, having so much fun. Now she doubted whether he was even attracted to her. Maybe he just loved his power over her. Maybe she should have told him what he meant to her and laid off criticizing his habits. She yearned for him, now that he was probably coming to his senses: obviously she was too old for him.

Khalid had a reed pipe for outings. Lazy improv concoctions floated from the orchard. His accidental notes transported her beyond the labyrinth of their relationship. The date palms were too dense to make out his silhouette, but she could see his music charm a kitten out of a pot. She chuckled, watching the kitties wrestle in the grass. A Chartreux brother kitten teased the others, then came and settled in next to Olivia for the mysterious concert from the twilit field.

It was tough in the underbrush. Another gray kitty chased a moth in the grass. Their mother, the sweetest cat, had been hunted down by the wild ones. There it was again, the loving one got offed.

Green eyes glowed in the bush. The wilder cats didn't dare come closer. They spied and waited under plants. How could love not be a survival skill?

Maybe the point was to die. Wasn't that what Greek heroes wished for, to die a valiant death? She could do without the violence, though.

Now smaller and higher, the Moon drained into the field, outlining every edge and transmuting lower matter. Earth's shadow touched the edge of the silvery ball. The eclipse. She wished she could distill Khalid's music into her loveoid sub stance, under standing...a position under matter where consciousness resided... She had to meditate on potentia. The loveoid would crystallize.

Khalid's vibrations wafted over the terrace. In the sky, Earth's shadow crept up on the Moon like a dark cloud. But there was no cloud in the sky: the eclipse was here. The world's shadow blotted out the brilliance of the Moon. Night enveloped the farm. Olivia was mesmerized. She'd lived in cities all her life. She'd never seen a lunar eclipse.

The kitties took advantage of her preoccupation and bombarded the house.

"Hey!"

Inside, they split up, one disappearing under the table, another making for the bedroom.

"Naughty kittens!" She scrambled after them like a lunatic.

The Key

Scientific research at the University of Cambridge shows that part of the human genome originated in plants and was transferred by micro-organisms horizontally, as opposed to vertical transfer of DNA from parent to offspring through heredity. "We may need to re-evaluate how we think about evolution," says Dr. Alistair Crisp.

ON THE COUCH, Khalid reached for his phone and pulled up a video. "Here's my friend's wedding."

Hundreds of Arabs paraded behind a fat bride clad in a flossy white burqua sitting atop a white bull. "That's the meat."

"Poor bull."

A squeaky clarinet cranked out a repetitive tune to accompany the exodus. It grated on Olivia's ears.

"My friends are getting married," Khalid said. He fast forwarded to the wedding feast, where the women were sequestered in their own courtyard. In the other courtyard, the men danced with each other in the dirt.

Olivia couldn't feign interest and went into the kitchen.

"My family is coming on Saturday," he called.

"Your family!" This really was turning into a

nightmare.

"My mother will bring lamb and some spices. You better clean the house tomorrow."

He found it natural that housework should fall on woman. Olivia had spent years working in the service economy without ever exercising basic housekeeping skills. It was bound to come around at some point. God forbid he should go all helpless in bed again. She weighed these obstacles against the man as she made her way to the bedroom alone. New Moon darkness left a spangle in the sky. *The stars are my eyes.* She watched the Milky Way until Khalid came around the outside of the window and bolted the shutters. Then he entered through the kitchen door and locked them in for the night.

In the middle of the night, the scream of the cats awoke her. Khalid lay silently sleeping. Could her lover be her man, her husband? The sacred word rolled off her lips. The one who would honor her forever. The one who meant everything and could turn her into nothing.

In the morning, she heard Khalid's footsteps in the living room. The sound of the shutters being opened, more light streaming in. He was up early. When she went outside, she found her favorite fluffy black kitty sprawled on the terrace, stiff. "Fluffy!" She picked him up and headed for the trash.

"Go around the house. Don't come in here with that cat."

"It's dead."

"Who knows what it has."

In shock, Olivia went around and laid the dead cat in the bushes for the land to take back. When the cats crawled into the bush to die, you never smelled a thing, the worms, slugs and insects devoured the carcasses so fast.

Trying to respect Khalid's culture, Olivia found a rag under the sink. A mountain range of dust collected on the black cloth. She cleaned for this man who surrounded himself with these objects...and she refused to compete with mere objects, careful not to topple anything. The dust got pushed around and landed on the surfaces again. So much organic matter behind the cabinet and inside the shelves! Olivia gave up using a rag. The only thing that worked was the sponge. She had to rinse it off after each surface.

"I don't use a vacuum cleaner." Khalid opened the closet. "I use a broom...why do you have to use electricity to sweep your floor? It doesn't make sense. You need to sweep out the negative energy."

She took the dust pan and broom and swept the particles off the living room rug. Tiny pieces of lives, now without significance, raw hopes finally extinguished: her pile on the floor mounted. She pressed the dustpan to the floor next to the pile — perhaps as meaningful as her work at the lab — banged the dustpan on the side of the garbage can, picked up the sponge again.

Khalid folded the sheets while they were still wet to fit them on a very short clothesline.

"Are those going to dry?"

"Yes. Here, everything dries."

Next, he showed her how to clean out the spirits. He lit a bowl of sage and waved the smoke into the corners. When the whole house had been cleaned, he stowed the bowl under the sink. "Where's the dish soap?"

"We used it up."

Khalid stiffened. This would mean a trip to the supermarket.

Olivia was sure of one thing, Khalid never wanted to go out. Never mind that it was springtime. When they absolutely had to leave the house, he would pick up his keys, take stock of his possessions, look her over head to foot, and hand her the hijab. He said he made her cover so that the villagers wouldn't know he was hosting a foreigner.

Singing, *J'ai du bon tabac dans mon tabaquier*, a song from nursery school, he double locked the front gate. He dropped her off with a shopping basket in front of a supermarket, its stone steps worn down by thousands of feet. She went off, yearning for a man who didn't want to be seen with her on the street. She finished the shopping and then met him back at the car.

But Olivia didn't experience Khalid's full charm

until he went and hid in his car around the block. Then there was the obligatory stop at the halal butchery, which Khalid handled himself, Olivia waiting in the car around the corner, he so did not want to appear in public with his older woman.

With the mythology of this arid land complete, they went home. Khalid looked in the bags. "You don't know how to love."

"Oh no! I forgot the soap," Olivia said.

"Is that your Alzheimer's?" Khalid exuded impatience.

"Allah! Do you understand English?" Olivia said, looking at the crack in the ceiling. "Why is Khalid angry about the things you have given him?" She went to work in the garden, then came back, hoping he'd forgotten about it and saw her as a dream again. She tried to make it up to him, cooking for the fourth night in a row while he played his lute.

He could be nice for a while. Then, "You didn't take out my plate! You took yours, and left mine on the table. I told you not to do that, and you went around me.

She tried to remain charming. It took enormous energy to keep it up. In Khalid's language, Olivia had disrespected him. In her language, he'd dissed her. If there was a happy medium in this doomed relationship, she didn't know where it was. There must be a way out. She prayed for an opportunity to escape.

When he was drained of his power, he vented on
woman. "It's not your role!" he lectured.

"Roles don't come easy to me."

"It shows."

Reduced! One link in the chain of slavery. "How
can I play a part when I'm after the truth?"

"When did you become so jaded?"

His temperament would suck the life out of her. *I
see why your colleague didn't love you* still rang in her
ears. So now Khalid didn't love her? *Please, God,
show me where he hides the keys.*

Khalid pulled on his gardening gloves. "I told my
family not to come this weekend."

A wave of relief.

Then doubt. When would he have told them? His
phone was still in the bedroom. She suspected his
family was never coming in the first place. It was all,
all a lie.

The Real Terrorists

With an increase of three degrees, the average drought in Central America would last 19 months. In northern Africa, 60 months—five years. In the United States, the areas burned each year by wildfires would sextuple.

OUT OF THEIR TRENCH COATS, the top twenty relaxed into neutral decor designed to camouflage gray lizards settling on rock.

The head of Trident kept his bomber jacket on. His face looked pale. Mutations were tricky.

"Let's be realistic," the chairman was saying. "It just happened with Zika."

The spread of microcephaly upward from Latin America to Afghanistan had stumped pharmaceutical logic. Scientists had only been able to ascertain the obvious: the brain stopped growing, so the skull stopped growing. Was it that the body stopped digesting certain enzymes and started photosynthesizing? No one knew how viruses caused mutations. And this new one, with all seven cases affecting extremely prominent business leaders — their own peers.... Beads of perspiration graced even the most reptilian of the corporate elite.

The room erupted in a hysteria of indignation: *So*

why is it only hitting the corporate elite?

A terrorist virus?

People will be dying at thirty-five again.

As they did throughout history.

We're a blip.

The gavel. "Gentlemen. Please." The initial panic gave way to cool analysis. "We're not there yet. There's no question of the human race devolving. Everything is under control."

But Desprez from Sanifree Pharmaceutical gave a worrying update on the loveoid.

"You *lost* a woman doctor in a hospital?" Roger the Brit glowered. "I told you so. Where is she! This mutation's hit our boardrooms. We're facing a direct biological threat."

Luther pulled his jacket tighter, an alarmed look in his eyes. "I'll find her, if I have to do it myself."

"Order!" the chairman said. "It's not going to be so easy this time."

Desprez from Sanifree practically yelled over his mic. "She's not lost. We talked to her yesterday. The research is underway, with your generous support."

Heads turned to the CEO of Trident. Luther pulled a clownish grimace, the hallmark of his last round of plastic surgery. "We always live up to our word: Trident will continue to back her research, as long as it's kept out of the media."

"Why keep it out of the media?" Shalom liked to debate, a hobby he exercised in a daily game of solitaire, as owner of most of the world's newspapers.

Desprez leaned into his mic, "... will wonder why we didn't put up this much funding for the Zika virus."

"Et alors?" said a mogul from Zug.

"The Zika virus affects everyone," Luther said, suddenly an expert. "This mutation is only hitting the elite."

"It's risky. Give me a few other options. I'll probably go, eh, not really, and then I might explore this one," Shalom prodded. "I mean, just because the so-called one percent is at risk, it has to be kept under wraps?"

"Correct," the Italian aristocrat agreed. "What usually happens when the rest of the world finds out they have spent their life savings on the ruling class?"

The business leaders twirled their pens and talked to each other. *The ROW will try to revolt whatever we do.*

Desprez noticed his mic, "...loss of its leadership."

The chairman added, "That means a shrinking economy." With those last words, he had their attention. "I guess I should have led with the end to growth in the first place."

The last lizard opened one eye, his gray Armani tie spread over the agenda. "What?"

Shalom leaned forward. "He thinks reliable

consumers mutating back toward their plant ancestors might interfere with growth."

Indignation flared around the table: *A drop in consumption could be expected. Simple Economics 101, supply and demand.*

"Can I steer the discussion back to immediate practicalities," said the chairman. "How do you propose justifying so much money to cure a disease ONLY affecting our species, so to speak?"

"OK, we keep that last part out of the media," Shalom said.

"Fine, then," said Luther, ever the talented manipulator. "Let the public think everyone is at risk."

It's not rocket science.

We leak our story. Journalists write it up and hit the bars.

The news scares the world to its knees.

The chairman hammered the table. "Everyone in favor of using the press to spread the scare, raise his hand." He stopped counting. As always, everyone was comfortable with terrorizing through the media, at least where 'everyone' glided within a narrowly circumscribed passage from White House to Wall Street. "Choirs of angels."

Shalom went about composing tomorrow's news. "For every added degree in temperature, the virus multiplies ten times faster. With this killer unchecked, the population in 2050 is projected at only five billion."

No doubt in a matter of months, they would eradicate the mutation triggered by this eight-million-year-old extremophile virus.

Octopus

Never lie to an older woman. She'll know.

WORLD FALLING APART around them, Khalid was barely getting by. It was too hard to make ends meet. The smallest disagreement could explode everything. He'd fight until he forced her to fight back, a wet blanket on their bedroom life.

"Is this why you don't have a wife?"

Anger mollified by unworthiness, he'd hang his head in shame. He folded inward, divided against himself. He just didn't deserve to have fulfillment. "I'm not nice."

Ashamed of his instincts, but unable to master them, he farmed with compulsive abandon.

Lying awake, Khalid asked her, "Why are you crying?"

Tears rolled quietly down her cheeks. "I'm sad that we can't be together forever."

"Stop crying," he commanded.

What could she tell this young stud of twenty-seven? She'd never fall for it at her age.

Khalid still in bed well after noon, she searched the bathroom: no keys. She tiptoed around the house looking under furniture, then sat with her eyes closed visualizing the keys.

"You're too heavy," he said from bed, falling deeper into debt with himself.

Maybe, she thought, making her melancholic a cabbage salad. Deep *was* heavy. All that water to hold up. With the sun on the surface broken.

"Smells good."

What an octopus he was. Changing colors all the time. She remembered his other selves, now that he was no longer deep with her. He shut her out with lies, expecting her to swim with him to the surface. Seaweed dangled from her foot.

Wasn't that the deal? she thought, hiding around the block from the supermarket. She'd known from the beginning, what they were chasing didn't exist. She'd only played along because he didn't know it yet. She'd even told him; he didn't listen, eyes wide shut at twenty-seven, still believing people could live up to myths from the sky. She would fight off reality as long as she could. When there was nothing left to leave up to his imagination, her young stud would get bored. Come to his senses. See her for who she was, and chuck her under the tractor.

So it shouldn't hurt when the expected occurred and dreams dissolved into familiarity. She wasn't going to stop loving him because he didn't want to be a dream. Although, she didn't think it would happen because she only got one soda at the supermarket instead of two, like he had specifically asked.

"I wasn't thirsty."

"It's like you stood me up."

"It is not." A silent lamb floated in the sky. Sometimes he was like a child who never learned to act in ways that would win approval. She got into the car. "I'm here."

"And you insist. You don't listen." An indignant display of knavery.

"I didn't want to waste a whole soda."

"It's like we said we were going to meet around the corner, and you left me standing in the street!" He kept getting his way, making her focus on him to feel his power over her.

Olivia clung to the notion that if only she tried hard enough, her Khalid would grow up. It seemed the only path. Her life was being reduced to one dimension—she dressed, worked, cooked and made love in ways that pleased her keeper. Khalid had forgotten his marital ambitions, but did encourage her to an extent. He was, on occasion, nice, after which Olivia blamed herself for the times when he was not.

She jumped at each sign of displeasure, her self-esteem so hinged on his approval. She brought him another beer. Her legs wobbled under the imbalance.

"You burned the meat."

"It's not burnt." She courted failure.

"I say it is."

She'd blown it.

"Come here."

She could feel her throat constrict, feet automatically carrying her closer. Her passion shrank to self-loathing.

Khalid was walking around the bed, yanking the sheets. "I don't have sex with people I don't love," black with a shrinking white dot. "Take off your dress."

She stood before Khalid in her bra and panties.

"Turn around."

She hesitated, doubting he was even conscious. He could take, but gave out nothing of himself, as if he had no more self to give.

"Do it." And he took her hips in his hands, startling her. Inspecting her rear, he adjusted her panties. Her back to him. "Do as I tell you. Understand? Bend over."

Olivia bent over the bed.

"Good girl." Khalid held her from behind. His hand reached inside her bra. "Head down." He pushed her shoulders to the mattress. He spread her legs with his knees, pushed into the warmth. *"Ah, oui."* With a jerk of his knees, he spread her legs further apart.

She moaned.

"You like it. Naughty girl. The curtains are open. Everyone can see you."

"What are you doing?"

"Just the head."

A chill ran throughout her body as he caressed nerves she didn't know she had.

"A little more." He caressed her butt and smacked it. Her hold on him tightened. *"Oui. Ah, oui."* Smack. Heat dripping onto the sheets.

*

The birds were starting to tweet. You could never really go backward. This was just a new layer to get through. Her heart battled with her head over whether to lie still or make a move.

Khalid's chest rose and fell. He snored from deep within inebriate slumber. This small event filled Olivia with hope and sorrow.

She rose without a sound, and snuck into the bathroom. His jeans were hanging on the hook. The ones he'd worn with her in the fields. A flash of memory, laughing with him until they cried. They had been so close. Her body contracted with pain at the thought of separation. She checked the pockets: a list in neat curling Arabic, a receipt, and a telephone number. A younger woman?

Conflicting emotions raged within. The thought of his being unfaithful on top of everything else sent her into fear. She just didn't feel she could count on a younger man. Her responsibilities gnawed at her. She had a job to do.

Olivia looked all over the bathroom again. *Where are the keys!* Getting down on all fours, she inspected the vent and opened the panel for the pipes, only cobwebs. This was insane. They had to be here.

She ran her hand along the bottom of the sink. Her fingers brushed a slight indentation. A metallic object fell out. Before they clattered to the tiles, Olivia caught the keys.

Chain of Command

Plants and humans share a common genetic past. Nearly two billion years ago, they were the same single-cell organism. Humans developed a central nervous system to integrate information. Plants did it without a brain. Humans and plants exchange carbon dioxide and oxygen with each other...

— *Director of the Manna Center for Plant Biosciences, Tel Aviv University*

THE DILEMMA EBBED from every chain of life, the loving perished, while predators stalked the food chain, chain of command, blockchain...

On a visit to Trident Fuel's West Coast headquarters, Trident's chief executive officer was fuming over the fact that Trident had to lower its oil production. "Rephrase that immediately!"

"Say what?" the communications officer asked, adjusting his black glasses.

"Say oil production will have peaked by 2022, for God's sake. Don't you people know how to write? You have a B.A. from..." Luther cornered the communications officer with a stream of verbal diarrhea, an affliction that had become more pronounced over the past few weeks.

Trapped in the deluge, the communications officer gagged an apology and closed the door. It was the last long-winded monologue anyone would ever hear from the oil magnate.

The next morning, when Luther's secretary knocked, there was no answer. She knocked again. Nothing. A naïve feeling of mild trepidation squeezed her chest. He hated being interrupted. She slowly opened the lacquered door in case Luther was on the phone. She peeked inside, never imagining the horrifying scene she was to witness.

Travel at Dawn

Attacks coordinated from the capital left one hundred and thirty dead on a high-speed train, and thirty-one killed in a bus station bomb attack. Of the 5000 jihadists estimated to have escaped to Europe, 94 were returned.

THE LEAVES GLINTED in the orange dawn. Olivia set off to undo what might have been, just like 'the clod and the pebble' never married. She trampled down the dirt road in her hijab, artifact and briefcase camouflaged in a grocery bag. Her mind raced. *Survive.* Everything would be fine now that she was free. Khalid's smile came to mind. She suppressed the memory. *Don't look back.*

Halfway to town, she heard a motor. She kept her eyes on her freedom, as if not looking would make the vehicle go away. She prayed it wasn't Khalid's Renault. There was nowhere to hide, just a thin path on the side of the road, and then a plane of cracked Earth. Her body cast a long purple shadow on the cracks. Her shadow rippled over the wrinkled Earth seemed to have the answer.

Suddenly, she understood what it wanted her to do to *survive.* Olivia doubled over and slowed her gait. She checked her shadow, *good:* now it was that of a grandmother permanently hunched from decades of picking zucchini flowers. Her shadow wobbled like a lump of clay.

The truck gained on her without slowing. Staggering along at a crawl, she followed the shadow of the grandmother. The old woman was invisible. The vehicle passed: red, not Khalid's.

In town, she found the bank. The cash machine spit out 240 dinars, its limit. The bus came soon after. She was glad it was almost empty. They rolled off through the countryside.

After two transfers and a snack, Olivia disembarked into a crowded street. She took a deep city breath. *I made it to*...she couldn't pronounce the name. Jagged ramparts timelessly guarded the old city against invasion from the sea. How did the ancients move those heavy stones? She caught a glimpse of blue water through an arch. Castle-top arrow slits encircled the medieval fortress. A starburst of palm trees rustled in the breeze.

Relying on her broken Arabic, Olivia persevered. She got lost in the busy winding streets on her quest for test tubes for the samples she would extract from the relic. She trudged on. Finding the equipment she needed would be a feat.

Other pedestrians became infrequent. The smell of figs melting in the sun quelled her thoughts. A fruit vendor convinced her that the hospital supply shop was behind the old hammam, embedded in the labyrinthine streets over to the right. She peered into the narrow passageway for pedestrians and maybe a donkey. She wasn't sure. You could easily get lost in such a maze. Was she supposed to walk alone along that abandoned section of the wall? Some of the houses had fallen down. She watched her shadow moving along the stones, carefully placed without the use of mortar, now craggy in patches with plants growing in the crevices. The 'wall', more like a long, thick building sloping gently upward forty feet, had rocks sticking out where staircases had crumbled. The dark shadows cast on one pile of rubble made it look startlingly like a mother holding a child. Her hair stood on end. Olivia stared at the crags as she walked past. The perspective changed, and it was just a pile of stones. She laughed at herself and pressed on.

Olivia hobbled up the medieval alleyway, feet sliding around in shoes over cobblestones. This was the way they'd said. These alleyways were starting to all look the same. She stooped into a spine of ancient arches connecting the building walls on either side of a narrow passage. More arches with trapezoidal stones, curves separating, connecting, conducting, grounding millennia of electricity running through their stone marrow. Arch after arch spanned the alleyways, buildings holding each other up as if spirits summoned back to life passed through petrified vertebrate. The path narrowed further and sloped upward, turning into a staircase. The walls on either side closed in as she climbed the last stair. Olivia ducked under a brilliant bougainvillea and came around the corner of a mosque.

The holy building was shaped like a ziggurat, each floor smaller than the one below. A giant tree gave shade to the whole square. She stopped at its twelve-sided fountain, and tried to get her bearings. There was the hammam, with the circle pattern in the windows forming six-pointed stars. The shop couldn't be far now.

Her shadow glided over the hammam's heavy wooden doors with rounded off tops, and the ground-floor windows ensconced in iron grills. She came to a green sign. She was unable to read the Cyrillic writing, but recognized the pharmacists' serpent and staff. The medical supply shop.

A mystic was shuffling a deck of cards outside the shop. "Lady scientist, get your reading!" the psychic called from her veils. "What you seek is in the last place you look."

Olivia hurried past and climbed the staircase up to a balcony with a view of the Seagate. Such grand construction, impossible to tear down even without government protection. With a jangle of bells, Olivia opened the door. She hurried in and bought their last kit.

Sore and tired, Olivia walked down the avenue

with her purchases. She headed in the direction of the sunset. Nothing mattered in that ethereal light. A maze of little-navigated alleyways wound through the terrain. Archeological pits laced with sweet smelling hay lay open under a giant tree. Stone roofs resurrected from abandonment walled off the sea. She passed one yard full of women roasting coffee, another with young boys scrambling after bottle caps, and at last, came out on a broad avenue with square trees.

Bodies clad in loud colors bobbed down the middle of the street. Their scent elicited a chain of memories that wafted to the outside of the mind. She joined the procession. A blessed calm settled over her. Finally a role she could play. A pedestrian.

The street was cast in purple shadow. Voices chanted. A honking car with flags flying from the windows crept forward. A troop of sloshed soldiers with machine guns up ahead sang,

> *"We are free men who are not afraid.*
> *We are the secrets that never die.*
> *And we are the voice of those who resist."*

The *manifestation* swept her up. As she marched with the demonstrators, she felt her connection to humanity's collective soul. This was what mattered, food, clean air and water. Love of life and Earth. Her worries dissolved into the elation of larger

purpose. The farmers had descended from their
fields by the thousands. The city was revealing the
sum of the past in this equivocal present. The
demonstrators carried signs, with an occasional
picture of a starving person in feudal garb. One
placard showed photos of foreclosures, another had
suicide victims. Their tents lined the sidewalks.
Ahead rolled a tractor with three field hands,
shouting about the drought. *Food!*

Farmers were an endangered species. So many
other factors affecting agricultural production
were beyond their control. Drought. Flooding.
Sandstorms. When their emotional wellbeing didn't
depend on the weather, it hinged on the whim of
government. And this one had apparently closed the
door.

Now she walked beside the car, driven by a
bearded man yelling at his wife. The woman cried
patiently at his side, tears darkening her turquoise
headscarf.

An army-green helicopter flew overhead. The
sound grew to a deafening roar. The copter raised a
cloud of dust. First she heard the screaming. Then,
everyone was running. She ran. A tear gas bomb
flew overhead. It hit a sign and broke open over the
crowd.

Olivia coughed and held her breath. She ran past
an official from the Ministry of Propaganda, who
was telling everyone to stop it. He blared through a

megaphone, hardly audible with the helicopter overhead fanning the flames.

The people grew angrier.

Coughing and sputtering, Olivia rushed toward a doorway. She escaped into a corridor and hurried into a bookstore. She landed in the magazine section. Outside the window, the figures in the street were barely visible behind yellow and gray smoke.

She milled through the bookstore pretending she was looking for a newspaper. Her eyes skimmed the headlines: *As extremophile cases threaten to spiral out of control, New York raises virus threat alert level.* The article made Olivia's blood boil.

> *...The move will usher in a governmental lockdown of cities and unilaterally bar visitors to prevent worldwide contagion.*

They would aggravate the virus! They could trigger a pandemic. The only danger was a few scattered mutations. There was no evidence that the mutation was contagious at all. It affected isolated people of a certain psychopathic disposition. The article didn't mention numbers, just, "Since August, at least 64,000 Americans have died of the flu." The flu! That many died of the flu every winter. Totally irrelevant, yet carefully worded. It was hard to see through their terrorist campaign. "How irresponsible." This would only spark fear, the opposite of a loving state. Terror was fertile ground for the mutation.

She turned the page and gasped. Her photo under the headline, *Missing Scientist.*

She put her sunglasses back on.

Extremovirus

The virus is at its fiercest in New York, with close to half a million confirmed cases on Friday, according to the latest figures from the Extremovirus Tracking project. Across North American countries 1,932,723 people have contracted it in the past day, accounting for nearly 43 percent of the disappearances.

HER SCREAM RESOUNDED in the corridor. The superintendent found the secretary with her back to the CEO's office door, both hands covering unbelieving eyes.

"What happened?!"

She tugged her skirt into place. "It's nothing," she convinced him. "I saw a mouse. It ran over there." Once he was gone, she forced herself into the office. She leaned back against the door, unable to comprehend what on Earth had happened to her boss. Although resilience and flexibility were her top qualifications, this was out of bounds. Disgust yielded to anger.

Seven minutes later, she had a cleaning company on the phone. A knock came at the door. Within seconds, the secretary was back out in the hallway shouting at the communications officer. "No press!

What planet are you on?" Half an hour later, she had their 2000 employees out in the street, and the world headquarters closed 'due to fire hazard'.

Only the secretary and the head of security remained in the building. She decided to let him in on the secret. He stood there staring at Luther for a full minute.

The secretary paced up and down. "We have to get him out of here."

"Unbelievable."

"Could doctors bring him back enough to at least get some passwords out of him?"

"Forget about it. Especially once his family finds out."

"Why not?"

"They might want to put him out of his misery. Euthanasia is legal here, as is assisted suicide."

As secretary to the director, she actually felt for Luther, with a kind of love that wouldn't let her do the obvious. "How do you know?"

"It's my job to know. Oregon is the continent's euthanasia capital."

"Christ. This is just too weird."

"It's actually quite normal. It's legal in several countries: Washington, Colorado, Vermont, Montana, DC, California, Belgium, the Netherlands, Luxembourg, Colombia. Assisted suicide is legal in Switzerland, Germany, Japan, Canada..."

"This is insane."

"It's still illegal in New York."

"Then, we have to get him back to his home country."

She paid a private removal company the price of a house in the Hamptons to remove him discreetly. The office rug and furniture were replaced. A month later, a short article would run on page four of the *Financial Times* saying that he'd stepped down to spend more time with his family.

The plan had been to transport Luther by landscaping truck to a facility in upstate New York. The truck's cargo was pronounced a biohazard, and refused at the border.

Resonance

An interesting phenomenon occurs when different vibrations come into proximity. After a while, they 'sync up': they spontaneously self-organize and start vibrating together at the same frequency.

"A CONTINENT in denial," Olivia said, folding the newspaper. Outside demonstrators clamored. The store owner kicked a man out.

Olivia took cover in the foreign books section. The smiling eyes of the woman on a book cover shone from behind a funeral-black burqa. Olivia skimmed the titles, *Ten Very Common Myths about Arab Lovers*. She was surprised to see this heading in a guide book to euthanasia facilities. Only the beginning. Hôtel Dido was listed on page twenty-two under a photo of people signing up to die at the hand of a perfect partner.

Olivia peeked out at the street. The smoke was dissipating, crowd thinning. She spotted a row of red umbrellas and settled into the safety of a sidewalk café. There, she witnessed the last of the evening glow.

Her finger skimmed the drinks menu. "I'll have a glass of champagne, please."

"Yes, Madame."

"And a pen, if you have one." She relaxed into her chair. He found her a blue pen. Sitting on a terrace, unfettered, she doodled on the back of her paper place mat, and watched the angry tide and its parade. Banners, bearded men, covered women, overtaken by women in shorts, a fit woman in a mini halter — the minimalistic statement spoiled by a tag sticking out between her shoulder blades.

Olivia sipped her champagne and scribbled. Not so many headscarves, now that the police were getting into the fray...that good looking guy in the red headband really did let that heifer put her arm around him—was she the one with the job? Olivia looked away when she saw them coming toward her.

The heavy foreign woman was settling in at the next table with the younger Arab man in the headband. He banished the bliss with a sharp tongue, complaining that his drink was all ice. Next the sun was in his eyes. Missing all of Allah's gifts, yet frustrated for more. Khalid would have become like that. She wondered what he was doing while she sucked up all this freedom.

Glancing at the next table, a part of her missed Khalid's lectures. She actually yearned for the man who avoided the love part of the relationship. She remembered finally talking him into a café; he was shocked that he had to pay. Olivia sipped her champagne and added these to her list of faults.

Wasn't that blood flowing from her pen? She hoped some divinities would notice and make her plea worthy. Make it come true, leveled passion, seeping from the napkin onto striped chair under red umbrella...

The couple at the next table got up without so much as looking at each other. They walked across the avenue and disappeared into the bushes.

...she could no longer read her handwriting. It was something about love.

Khalid hadn't called. He must be angry. What did she care if he was angry? He was the one with slutty phone numbers in his pocket. She pulled out his list with the number and dialled it. A recording came on in Arabic followed by English, "Suicide Prevention Lifeline. For a consultation, press one..." She hung up in a fluster.

A farmer's life was harder than she'd thought. Just to be self-sufficient in the essentials for life, things we took for granted, food and clothes, shelter and fuel, hanging on to his land at all costs. When farmers couldn't fulfill this instinctual purpose, they felt despair. The paradox: what fulfilled the farmer also spelled failure, and could drive them to suicide.

The waiter came out with a tray of tall ice cream glasses held above his head. His Pascal Lushe cologne lingered in his wake. Olivia's stomach rumbled. She should order some dinner.

The disquiet had faded. The drones had stopped flying overhead. The demonstration had trickled to a few stragglers, the last pedestrians wandering off into the dusk. A deadening silence descended.

Where was that waiter? There was no one in sight. But no one. No other customers, not a car driving down the street. Olivia stood up. Where had everyone gone? Surely nightlife was happening here, of all places, on a spring evening. Olivia looked at her watch, nine fifteen p.m., then behind her. The door to the café was open, but there was no one inside.

"Hello?" she called as loud as she could. She walked to the back, no one in the kitchen. There was absolutely no one anywhere.

The realization that she was alone rendered her need for food more pressing. Dishes remained piled up on the metal countertops. In a panic, Olivia opened the refrigerator. A plate of goat cheese. She looked around. Of course, no one was watching. All at once, she felt utterly lonely. Where could everyone have gone? If they were dead, there would be bodies. Eating a slice of cheese, Olivia noticed her phone ringing. Khalid.

"Where are you, *Bébé*? I've been trying to call you for a long time." Khalid's voice was soft. "Don't worry about the things you said, *Bébé*. Everything's going to be fine."

"But…"

Amidst effusive apologies, possibly the last man on Earth promised he'd never do it again. He looked a little better, contrasted with the prospect of living utterly alone for the rest of her life. After talking to him for fifteen minutes, Olivia sighed and recounted her trip to the city.

Khalid sounded grateful. "When we're angry, we say things we don't mean. I understand. I've forgotten about it."

"Which 'things'?"

"When you said you wanted to break up."

"When I said...? But, Khalid, I didn't say—"

"I'm scared, too, *Bébé*. Is there anyone there with you?"

"No. It's spooky."

"I'll bring the truck. Stay there, *Bébé*. Don't leave."

Olivia's adrenaline was pumping as she waited in the café. Soon she would no longer be alone. The streetlights shone on the thick bushes lining the avenue.

A motor whirring in the distance.

Khalid's truck rolled down the Avenue Habibi in the wrong direction with Wahad in the back. He swerved to the right, and almost hit one of the thick trees obstructing the road.

Olivia stood up to get a better look, astonished at the outgrowth of vegetation encroaching on the avenue. Khalid stopped in the middle of the street and left the door open. A wave of relief engulfed her. Of course she loved him. She was afraid she was going to die of it. Who else could appreciate him as he was, unsuppressed, free of brainwash... She had cornered the market for this man.

His shadow preceded him. His silhouette blotted out the sky. A corsair elegance, that had caught her off guard. Their differences seemed precious under new circumstances; she was glad his DNA existed.

So resumed their situationship.

Wahad wagged his tail and almost jumped up on her. Khalid drew her into his arms, whispered, "Never leave me, *Bébé*." She could feel his desire erupting and capsized into his male-lava scent. Their lips touched, his arms strong around her waist as she sank into his kiss. Was it really so quiet, or were they falling deep into oceanic origins, the first man kissing the first woman....he rose to his surface, becoming lighter, and held her face in his hands, dark eyes inviting.

They clung to each other and stared at the wildwood lining the avenue.

"Where is everyone?" Khalid asked. "Are they in jail? Will they come for us, too?"

"We're still here, Khalid." Olivia held his gaze. "It must be love."

"There's your proof," Khalid said. He handed her Wahad's leash. "Wait here."

"Khalid!"

He yanked his toolbox out of the truck and then

led her a few doors down to an entryway.

"What are you doing?"

"What do you think?" He looked at her sidewise, brow arched, and then worked on the keyhole. "Kidnapping you."

The chill that usually ran down her spine when he said that was now gone. She watched his muscles tighten as he dismantled the door.

Soon, all three of them were climbing up the stairs, up, up, to the top floor, past the penthouse, maids' quarters, and up a narrow, winding staircase to a breathtaking roof. The Milky Way lit up the darkness. "We should be quick," as if they had to be making love under the stars, before someone sicked capital punishment on them, and turned the empty little coastal town into an economic miracle.

She folded her arms. Streets below, etched in attempted organization, waited for no one. Not a car, no men, no women, no other possibilities, just Olivia and Khalid. His arms were around her again under the twinkling stars. He drew her into his world, illuminating and tugging at her soul.

Her skirt fell to the rooftop, followed by his jeans, irrelevant now, the usual restrictions no longer applying so high above the abandoned avenue. They rejoiced in the new solitude, exploring the depths of hope as their spirits expanded out over the empty city, and then hovered peacefully around their bodies, now lying spent.

*

With nothing to brush up against or conform to, they grew bigger. They burst from constrictions, and deepened into an inner dimension.

Olivia's list of required faults grew longer as she thought about a man who played music she couldn't understand. She wanted a man whose face, with hooked nose and sculpted goatee, had that rare, marauding beauty that had been refined out of Western man, a magnificence that demanded its due compensation from the world. She wanted to hear the soft orders of the man who finally met her in the bathtub after all the bubbles had popped and said, "You used the wrong soap."

No need for clothes in the summer heat, Khalid's skin turned a deeper bronze. Olivia noticed he was following her around these days. Whereas he used to leave the women's work to her, now he didn't mind accompanying her inside the supermarket on food hauls. There was no one to sell the goods.

The streets suffused in an unshakable calm, they loaded the bags into the trunk together. She might be missing havoc in New York, but here, she was at one with Nature. The warm caress of the summer night on Olivia's skin was so intimately relaxing, she was here and nowhere else.

In the hot summer breeze, their differences

chipped off and blew away. Because she'd dispensed with her clothes, or perhaps because there was no one else to be with, Khalid seemed content by her side. Now they could see. They had mistaken their true selves for the roles they'd played. Now they fell deeper into their bond.

Six Shocking Ways Arab Lovers Will Make You Better in Bed

With their respective speeds of electrical oscillations in the various brain regions, Gamma, theta and beta waves, resonate to produce human consciousness.

THE STREETS WAITED below in final calm. "What happened?" Khalid asked, as if awakening from a dream. He observed the landscape with the mystified look of someone logged in to the quantum field. Here was another universe, one of the billions that might have sprung up at some random obstacle, to blossom into more possibilities. He reached for Olivia.

"I don't know."

Although there was no other life-form in sight, they felt like they were being watched. Sometimes they talked without knowing what they were saying, listening to each other's voices.

*

Olivia ran her nails along his chest. "Look at you! You're all bronze. You're handsome." *And so hard.*

"You're beautiful, *Bébé,* all white." He slid her string to her feet. He opened her legs and put his finger inside. *"Ah oui."* He bit his lower lip. "You're all...*rose."*

His eyes drew her out. Her moans collided with his. The static escalated until she couldn't stand it anymore.

"Cries Bébé, cries."

She watched his reflection in the mirror take control, turning her around. He tipped her butt toward his pelvis and mounted. Her eyes widened. Olivia understood why such an intrusion was illegal in some countries. Not that there was anyone besides Khalid to enforce anything. She glimpsed his face as he awakened deeper sensations in her than she'd ever felt. His eyes locked in intimate connection with her eyes. His body sizzling hot, leaning into hers. He opened her further and rode the wave to completion.

They faced each other again, sweating and spent.

He looked puzzled. "I guess you didn't enjoy what we just did."

"Yes, I did." The climax had been profound ...she knew how to use her hand.

"Then we're going to do it again."

*

Olivia tiptoed around, until she heard him stir in bed, and then boiled water for his coffee, half-full, two sugars. If she didn't make it right, he would dump it, turn on the hot water, fill up the cup with tap water, and add the instant and the sugars himself.

Hair tousled in the most adorable torrent, Khalid got up and followed her around. Olivia disappeared into the bathroom.

Khalid tried to follow her. "Why are you closing the door?" He asked, peeking in.

"You're cute, *Chéri.*"

He went nuts dominating her. "I'll kidnap you."

They met again at the coffee table, laden with a repast of French bread, jam, mango, kiwi, and coffee just right. Khalid exclaimed, *"Voilà* everything you need!"

*

At night, a healing calm awakened their bodies. All their rejected pieces were witnessed and accepted. They came together in a whole-bodygasm.

"You're a powerful man."

"Me, powerful?"

"You're able, that's your power." His love came from strength, rather than need, from a will to expansion rather than escape, "...not the kind of power over other people that leads to enslavement. I mean your real power, from the source. You transform Earth's seeds into food, your power makes things come true."

Encouraged to look beyond domination, he said, "*Chérie*, do you think I'm good for your work?"

She threw back her head. Her work? A distant memory.

"But can you work better when I'm around?"

She stole a glance at his profile waiting expectantly and remembered to care about the loveoid and the mysterious puzzle piece hidden here in North Africa. "You're an inspiration, *Chéri*." Exhausted, Olivia snuggled up to Khalid.

*

Khalid needed to be his own boss. His desire for personal freedom interfered with everything else in his life. For her part, Olivia also enjoyed the freedom of having less 'stuff' to take care of.

She had abandoned her work.

Khalid gave her his full attention. "What were you searching for?"

"A loveoid."

"A what?"

"Medicine to make people loving. It was a way to stop the mutation."

"Some survive." He held up his arms, living proof.

"Yes."

"We already know we need love to survive."

"I was trying to get competitive mammals to feel

empathy."

"They need their survival skills."

"Well, it was going to be for humans, who need to survive as a collective. Human predators can become abusive, fascist. Loving needs to become a survival skill." Olivia tied her hair in a knot. "It's a simple principle..." The mutation started at the core. But it couldn't find the core of those in love: lovers' centers were outside of their selves. Somewhere in between, in an ethereal sea of plasma, not in the body. The loveoid had to move the person's center to a field of energy outside of the self, where the mutant DNA couldn't travel.

"Ah ha." He arched his brow. The issue had become too big to see. "And you're sure this isn't an illusion? Your career seemed to depend on your loveoid."

They left off cooking and just had a light salad for dinner. Olivia squeezed a lemon over her plate. "Self-centered people focus on their own energy. It gets bogged down in their physical bodies. They're stuck with themselves. That's what makes them vulnerable to attack. I was going to derive the loveoid from biochemical processes in the brain of loving people under caring conditions."

Khalid leaned his chair back like a teenager. "Not a very smart idea."

"Not smart?" *You're jealous.*

Folk Remedies
Using Only Arab Lovers

Plants have evolved highly sophisticated defense mechanisms enabling them to repel predators by fabricating chemicals, but they cannot survive the human population bomb, according to the plant rights group PRGU...

HE REACHED INTO her pocket and pulled out a vitamin C. "No medicine, *Bébé.*"

How was she going to keep from getting sick? Lucky it was summer; just wait till he saw how pathetic she was in the wintertime. Was she a fool to think she could keep such a young man?

"I can cure," Khalid said.

He certainly had inspired her to exercise more. "How's that?"

"For gastritis, you eat protein, no carbs or sugar, or, even quicker, boil the skin of a pomegranate and drink the tea."

One time she tried it. It worked immediately.

"You see? Look at me. I don't even take vitamins. If you want your minerals to get absorbed, you have to eat dairy separate from meat and legumes, and never with coffee — no food with coffee." He hunched over his new lute and plucked a stream of illogical notes.

He was the flower of youth. Of course, he didn't need vitamins. But she tried separating dairy, and her favorite, eating the pectin of different colored apples to make her joints feel younger. For a sore throat, it was red-hot chili pepper and a string of lapis beads; for an earache, it was salt water and the hair dryer.

*

"Tu me plaît. Tu n'as pas de ventre."

"I don't have a tummy?" If that was all it took, she could have even less of one. She stepped up her abdominal workout.

The alarming calamity of the human situation evaporated in comparison to the improvement in their lives. Walking around without any clothes, eating with their hands, it was good. The absence of society left them in a place where love could ring true. Love moved beyond desire, no longer a beggar's need, but the sharing of an emperor's overflowing compassion.

"Let's go to Egypt, *Bébé.* I've never seen my home country."

Olivia scanned the placid cityscape, so crisp now that the smog had been retired. "I'd love to see the pyramids. Is there still a ship, and where will we get the gas to drive to the port?"

"We'll walk."

"It's way too hot to walk."

"When autumn comes, it will be cool enough. We'll catch the Friday ferry. We'll get married and have our honeymoon in Egypt."

*

The drought deepened. They waited it out in their corner of Anthropocene, living on canned goods and bottled water from abandoned supermarkets. A pack of dogs followed them from store to store. They opened dog food and fed them in the street.

The dry spell was followed by thunderstorms and Biblical flooding. This made it harder to feed the dogs. They built a raft out of an old garage roof.

Khalid fell ill.

Olivia shivered. "I thought I would be the one to get sick first. What is it?"

"I can't pee."

She repeated his maxim, "Keep it clean, and it will heal itself."

But he wanted her ass.

She listened to him cursing in the bathroom. "We have to find antibiotics."

Clothed in sunlight, they went to the Hôpital Wassila, with Khalid cursing all the way. They searched the pediatric ward.

"Why did you bring me here!" Khalid yelled at Olivia as she sailed through the emergency room doors and ransacked the drawers in an examination room for antibiotics. Khalid grabbed a bottle away from her. "Let me check the spelling."

"The spelling?"

"They didn't teach you *l'importance* of spelling? In ancient Egypt, it was forbidden to translate sacred texts because it would disable the spells." Khalid read aloud, enunciating every syllable's vibrational tone.

Olivia put her hands on her head. Her eyes came to rest on a pair of white shoes under the curtain that divided the room in half. The shoes were walking toward them. The curtain undulated.

"May I help you?" a male orderly asked, coming around the curtain.

Khalid whirled around to face the man in green scrubs. *People!* "We were just looking for antibiotics — " Olivia stammered, suddenly aware that she wasn't wearing any clothes.

"*Oh Allah!*" Khalid yanked the curtain off its hooks and threw it over Olivia. "I told you!"

"No you didn't!"

"I said there might still be people."

"You did not!"

The orderly handed Khalid a hospital gown. He jumped into it.

Veil thrown over their non-separability, Khalid

and Olivia peered into the corridor. A nurse and a doctor walked by holding hands.

"We didn't think there was anyone else!" Khalid said.

"There aren't too many. Only a few couples, I'm afraid," the orderly said.

As they pieced together the orderly's story, Olivia's and Khalid's eyes met, staring into their bond as necessary as air.

Outside, they began to breathe freely again, until Olivia walked out into the street without pulling her hospital gown closed. "Oh whore!" Khalid exclaimed. The argument that ensued sucked the lifeblood out of her. After a day of defending her spiritual inertia, women and the educated class, it dawned on her that they were back on Khalid's farm. She'd hardly realized it. They didn't usually sit and argue on the kitchen floor, collapsing the whole summer into minutes.

"You refuse to see." He was holding onto her ears.

"It had nothing to do with your spelling."

"Yes, it did. See, for once! The eye isn't just for taking in. We project from the eye."

"You're crazy."

"Then what's the evil eye?"

"We don't have that."

"Oh, come on. Everyone has it. This is basic. The evil eye is the projection of a curse when someone sees something beautiful and feels jealous. Every country in the world has the evil eye except the United States?"

The fact remained: there were other people to rely on: now that she wasn't as necessary to his survival, he wanted to argue. He browbeat academic logic for distrusting the connection between Heaven and Earth. Then, government. Mayors who had no awareness of their power to join society with Heaven and Earth always brought chaos and natural disaster. Drought. Crop failure. Starvation, earthquakes, all because Heaven and Earth doubted the power of the mayor.

And Western science! Barreling everyone toward extinction. "Why save the upper class? Nature will take care. Love is all there is. Everything else is an illusion. You don't need a pill. Love is the seed. You're an authority. With your abilities, you could be a spiritual leader. Why don't you work on your own research. You don't need them. If you'd just act on your convictions, you could set in motion the kind of change that would really help."

The relic stared down at her from the kitchen shelf. Her work. She looked at him squarely. She knew she'd jinx him in bed, but she couldn't stop herself from saying it. "Khalid, there are still people to save. I need to do my research, and I can't do it on the farm."

"What!" Hadn't he gone to great lengths to help her find the truth...whether Olivia was there as a prisoner or willingly, and whether they agreed or not? "This is the perfect place for biologists. Everything grows in this sun."

With a rush of tears, they ended in each other's arms.

"Where am I going to find a centrifuge, test tubes...I need mice."

Khalid opened one eye.

A field mouse ran across the threshold. It stopped and stared at them and then scurried under a plank.

Man Destiny

"You think those dogs will not be in Heaven! I tell you they will be there long before any of us."

— *Robert Louis Stevenson*

THE TRANSFORMATION to love had happened outside of society. Now, there were others to rely on, and Khalid didn't seem to need her as much. Society was encroaching again, and their little utopia didn't quite carry over. The battle of the sexes was on.

People trickled back into the village; a surviving family member and his sweet wife had taken over the gas station. Khalid waited for Olivia in the truck around the corner from the supermarket, where you could buy a newspaper again. *The outside world had carried on!* When she arrived with the bag of shampoo, toilet paper and beer, he reverted to bullying.

All that time and energy, just to get to zero. Olivia shredded their last cabbage into a salad. A variation on yesterday's meal.

They no longer needed the permit, but they still needed the well. They drove to the nearest water. The river was evaporating. After days of fishing, Khalid managed to catch a small salmon. Birds circled above, watching Olivia scale the fish.

"It'll get better next year," Khalid said. He cooked the fish over an open fire, tucked the potatoes he'd dug from the red Earth into the coals. "Bring me another beer," he snarled.

Autumn came two months late. A cool breeze swept leaves across the courtyard. Drifters traipsed onto the farm. A half a bushel of peaches disappeared. One hungry vagabond had the nerve to show his face during the day. Olivia hid in the bathroom, and hoped he wouldn't do what he said he'd do if someone tresspassed on his farm.

Khalid growled like a bulldog, but the emaciated man went on pleading. She watched from the window, as Khalid ran to the shed, grabbed his scythe and chased the drifter off the land.

They worked separately that day, Olivia in the kitchen, Khalid in the courtyard. The red sun lurked behind the brush. It crouched lower like a wild animal.

Olivia feared the ideas that must have crept into Khalid's head. He could get a good ransom for his slave. Sitting outside the kitchen, she clutched her newspaper. Feline sentries guarded the courtyard. Her eyes had reached the bottom of the column without registering any meaning. He nicked the page.

"Hey!"

"And you read those lies." He sat down across from her with his arms folded, one eyebrow arched.

The loving perished first. The dilemma ebbed from every shore. "This story relates to my research."

"Stories!" He waited.

"Yeah, stories. I'm full of stories, from before your time."

"*Genre.*"

"Like this one." She held up the page. "This head of an oil company had allegedly quit to 'spend more time with his family, leaving a management void,' as if he would willingly give up all that power. Now he's disappeared." Olivia smoothed the newspaper out on the coffee table:

The chief executive officer of Trident Fuel made his last decision, in his hotel room in Oregon before he was found rooted to the carpet.

I'm sure there's another predator ready to climb to the top of the ladder."

"Maybe on the scale you can see."

"And *you* perceive another scale?"

"Why not? I tell you, *dogs* can hear notes on a higher scale."

"I know. I'm a biologist," she reminded him, newspaper blocking her face.

"Humph." He turned away from the Trident

article. "Let's hear our horoscope."

Scrutinizing him over the page, Olivia watched Khalid put his feet up on the coffee table.

"Seriously?"

Farming by Moon phase was one thing, but astrology. "You, you..." She tried to be nice. "Tell me you don't actually believe in that stuff."

He leaned back in expectation.

She read the Astro Twins take on the shituation,

You may have suddenly had to add some new functionality to your space: office, one-room schoolhouse, self-care meditation cave. This Monday, March 30, your co-ruler Mars will buzz into Aquarius, activating your domestic zone until May 12. The red planet hasn't visited this sector for two years, so don't be surprised if you're suddenly keyed up to make some big changes around Chateau Scorpio.

The newspaper sank to her lap.

He looked offended. "It always amazes me how few scientists acknowledge gravity." It wasn't a question of faith, but rather of expanding toward radiation. "All animals and plants reach for light. Hatchling sea turtles follow the Moon until they arrive at the sea. Fields of *tournesols* turn their heads to follow the sun across the sky..."

Olivia nodded doubtfully, unsure she'd even want

to go on living inside a giant mind with galaxies for neurons. She found it highly unlikely that she'd gravitated toward any particular constellation happening to brand the sky when she'd 'manifested on the material plane'. If she could make such an impression on the universe, she would have done it already in the lab.

Khalid sat with his spine straight, hands firmly planted on his knees and looked through her with an intensity that showed no sign of letting up. "After Christians burnt down the Library of Alexandria and suppressed the knowledge coming out of Egypt, your Western newspaper still can't sell enough copies without printing horoscopes."

It lay folded on the coffee table. "We're in World War III...*Chéri.*"

"You realized? With three eyes closed! *Laisse tomber.* You're safe here. I'm not a terrorist. I don't even like globalization."

He checked his phone, hopefully.

Olivia wondered what message could be making him so anxious. Another woman?

"Normally by now the work picks up."

....while he kept her from *her* work. Separation gaped. How quickly affection wore off. She had a sinking feeling he was plotting against her. He must have guessed her value on the market, now that there was one again. Her eyes wandered to the window with the shutters bolted shut.

Intelligent Life

Based on the observed behavior of the entities that surround us, from electrons to atoms to molecules to bacteria to paramecia to mice, bats, rats, etc., all things may be viewed as at least a little conscious. This sounds strange at first blush, but 'panpsychism' — the view that all matter has some associated consciousness — is an increasingly accepted position with respect to the Nature of consciousness.

— Scientific American

"HAVE YOU FOUND anything with all your silly research?" Khalid said from the doorway.

In Olivia's desperation to survive, she might have overlooked a few of his flaws. His callousness reminded her not to place too much hope outside herself. If there was any way to bring this situation into alignment, she would first have to look for fulfillment within. "Glad you brought it up. I need to get to the caves."

"What will you find there?"

"Clues." She looked at him squarely. "Traces of a top-secret, extinct civilization."

"A what?"

"The intelligent species that goes with that tooth, maybe one that inhabited Earth long before Homo sapiens arrived 300,000 years ago. Look, I can't stay here."

"You can't run off into the desert. You're a blonde woman alone. You'll be beaten and killed."

"I've got work to do."

"It's too hot. You won't be able to carry enough water."

"If I don't, everyone's going to die."

"Everyone where?"

"All over the world, important people, leaders..."

"We're on a self-sufficient, organic farm. I'm the only leader. You can save me."

"How organic is it?"

"These days, very. Pesticide is expensive. I'm not going to spend a fortune while the rest of the world lines up to euthanize. What do you need?"

Olivia stood there speechless.

"I'll get it, whatever it is."

"It's no use. The mission has already been compromised. I need a goddamned laboratory! I...I need human bodies that died experiencing love."

"If it doesn't have to be goddamned, we can do it here." He took her by the wrist and walked her to the shed. "Here's your lab, blessed by Allah."

"Thanks, but I can't...it's full of old stuff."

He was taken aback by the disrespect in her tone. "What old stuff?" He began to transport his collection of junk into his underground cellar, leaving only his most necessary tools leaning against the walls.

"Khalid, I appreciate what you're trying to do for me, but this won't work. I need equipment, refrigeration, a centrifuge, and human cadavers—"

"You can use animals."

"Animals don't love."

"Heh, is that what you think? Let me do the thinking." He searched his phone. "You believe Allah forgets who he is and becomes a stupid creature? If you love animals, you'll see that they love more than humans...here's a university selling its used lab equipment."

Khalid's optimism did eventually influence her, as he knew it would. He credited Jupiter's conjunction with his ascendant.

Boxed into the four walls of the shed, Olivia trembled at the thought of laying scientific foundations in the quicksands of superstition. She ran her fingers through her hair. "I don't know where to begin here."

"*N'importe*. Everything's a circle. It begins everywhere."

*

A week later, Olivia had a centrifuge and a Bunsen burner going. Her concoction bubbled in the makeshift lab.

"So you're looking for...," Khalid said, standing in the doorway.

"A loveoid."

"Allah! What is love?" His shoulders filled the doorway. He raised one arm and leaned his exquisite physique against the frame.

"Indeed," she said, looking at him through a jar of blue liquid. "To put so much hope outside of yourself doesn't seem healthy or wise. It sounds more like getting sick: touching, connecting, taking into your body, guarding jealously until love hardens into habit, and leaves you lonely again."

He stared at her blankly.

She swirled the liquid. "Look at this." She held up a test tube. "It's actually a plasmid with a gene on it that enables us to love. Love generates gravitational waves, subtle ripples in the fabric of space-time that pull the center of being outside the self."

"See? Gravitational waves," Khalid said.

She went on anyway. "Well, yeah. The first gravitational wave was identified by the Virgo detector located near Pisa, Italy. There are twin detectors in Livingston, Louisiana, and Hanford, Washington. They're trying to observe the signatures of extra dimensions in the ways that gravitational waves undulate through the universe. I just need the wave mechanism to move the center outside of the self, where the mutation can't affect it."

"Why are you telling me this?"

"You're the only one I can tell."

"Why?"

"You won't understand."

Khalid stroked his goatee. He turned his back on the shed, picked up a pine cone and chucked it at the fence. " 'Won't understand!' I understood *that*." Coming back into the lab, he said, "I understand. You think you're more advanced, but look where you're advancing. *I* can't tell *you*."

"Tell me what?"

"*You* wouldn't understand." Back turned, Khalid crossed his arms.

"OK, I'm listening. Tell me. I'll try to understand this time."

He looked up at the blank sky. "I can't tell you."

"Why?"

"You want to solve Nature. Here you finally get away from the dangerous element you work for. You see Nature recycling them. What's to fix? Saving the upper class? I know you're working for people who are against you. Why? *Vraiment*, it's you who won't understand."

Olivia distributed the test-tube contents into petri dishes and stacked them in the mini-fridge. She had been taught there was a certain way to do research, or it couldn't be done at all.... OK, in practice, things weren't so black and white. They were, in fact, the opposite: even the opposites themselves had turned out to be degrees of the same thing. No one could say where darkness ended and light began...

"You have enough. What could they give that's so important?"

There was the money and recognition on the bright pole — perhaps winning a Nobel Prize — and then on the dark pole, worrying that Khalid might guess the stakes and hold her for ransom. They were gradations of the same phenomenon; the existence of one depended on the other.

Rather than trying to shovel out the darkness of misapprehension, she'd have to open the shutters and let understanding shine in. "OK," she said, "maybe it's not so complicated." She followed him out into the courtyard and looked up at the clear blue sky. *Why save 'intelligent' life forms? They kill off the other animals and destroy their own habitat...* "I know you see it as funding to save the unworthy, but —"

"How much?"

"Just enough." *Seven billion!*

"If the loveoid works, maybe corporate oligarchs won't be such a bad lot."

"I'm telling you, submit to Nature. My mother got all her food and medicine from Nature. It's here for us. Why try to dominate it?"

"She's...not alive anymore?"

He looked at the sky.

Olivia remembered cleaning the house for his

mother's non-visit. Was this a lie, too? "I'm sorry."

"It was her time."

She put her arms on his shoulders.

"You see how I need a wife. Wouldn't you like to marry me?"

Olivia was dumbfounded. She wished she could believe in the domestic harmony he described. And while she had to admire his lofty ideals, she was sure she'd lose him in marriage. The familiarity would kill what was left of their love.

"We can stay on the farm. Look how beautiful the sun is today."

He really did seem to derive the deepest pleasure from home life. The spiritual love he was proposing had already transformed her. It hurt so much to resist his magnetism. She said it softly, "I have to get out of here."

"To go where? The caves? Then you're going to find what you're looking for?"

"Maybe. I'm supposed to research the ancient caves."

"Do you feel that's your purpose, or did they tell you to research the caves?" He shot her an accusatory look: she was trying to see a ball with calculus. She'd wandered off on all the tangents.

This time, she stared at the red sun.

"Fine. I'll take you there."

Animus

Scientific testing has produced no evidence to support astrology's premise that there is a relationship between astronomical events and phenomena on Earth.

THEY PARKED UNDER A FIG TREE and hiked in. The intense heat had melted Olivia's suntan lotion. The harsh terrain certainly wasn't offering any clues as to why a humanoid civilization might survive longer in this location than others. Scaling a rocky embankment, she was relieved to see the honeycomb of caves dotting a cliff wall across the cove. Their fatigue immediately forgotten, they scurried down the other side to the rocks on the shore. A family of kittens crept out of a cranny and escorted them across the hot sand to the water's edge.

"How are we supposed to enter the caves from here?" No one could climb over that crag to get down to the entrance.

"The only way there is."

"You're joking." Olivia shielded her eyes. The Mediterranean throbbed under a placid skin. The sun neared its zenith with its legion of reflections sparkling on the sea. Khalid had stripped off his navy blue shirt. Olivia flung her dress on the sand. A moment later, they were naked, wading into the turquoise. Their feet exploded the ribs on the bottom into clouds of sand. Little fish scurried away to join their school, then jumped from the water in a silvery arch.

Khalid jogged in slow motion, his feet stirring up clouds of sand. His back muscles flexed as he swung his arms. *All that farming paid off.* Her eyes drank in his chest, forgetting any threat to her freedom.

Olivia sucked in her stomach and ventured up to her waist in the cold water. She kept her fingers just above the surface. The sea drew the heat from her body.

Khalid dove in.

"Really?" A chill ran down her spine.

"Come on, it's refreshing," muscles springing to life, black hair flattened into a cap.

"Ha. Stay away." She hopped back. Her legs divided a school of tiny fish. Her feet pounded the water. A small white crab scurried into a hole on the bottom. Khalid was far out now, his skin luminescent against the glinting sea. She sank into the water back-first. Turning, she braced herself and plunged. She overcame the shock of the cold. Accepted the cold. Her arms sliced the water in exhilaration, bending for maximum resistance with each stroke. Her body glided through soft waves. She took in the pattern of light they made on the bottom. Refracted rainbows shimmered like a web of neural networks...so the world *was* a big mind after all.

An elongated cornetfish escaped her shadow darkening the turquoise. It darted into the sea grass.

Far behind Khalid, free-styling toward the caves, Olivia flipped onto her back and kicked up a white crest. Goosebumps spread across her limbs. A tingly feeling enshrouded her body. She counted the strokes, started over at a hundred.

Yellow rock against blue, Khalid was almost there. He pulled himself out and lay flat on a boulder, brown chest heaving. Olivia breast stroked into the middle of the inlet, paused to catch her breath. The water was calm, revealing the rocks on the seabed. They seemed to be moving with the soft undulation of the sea.

She heard a splash behind her.

Turning, she froze in horror. As much as it was possible to freeze without sinking, while suppressing the urge to scream. She stared back at a giant snake head. The thing was less than three meters away. It blinked its glassy eye as if from another dimension. She would sink. She swished her hands trying not to attract any more attention than she already had, thankful that at least snakes didn't have ears. The diameter of its neck was as wide as her hand. Was she hallucinating? A thought flashed, *With that thing guarding them, the caves might still be intact.* Olivia looked for the giant snake body that must be stretched out underwater, ready to wrap itself around her. All she saw was a large, dark disc as wide as an easy chair. Who sent this chimera? Its black, lizard eye blinked again, expanding the red and yellow stripes along its jowls and neck.

Over the crash of the waves she could hear Khalid laughing. "It's an old sea turtle."

"Oh my gosh!" she said under her breath.

The ancient creature plunged.

Olivia stuck her head under the glassy surface and opened her eyes, looking for the round giant. It should have been right in front of her. Instead, she only saw light blue turquoise in every direction. She came up, salt stinging her eyes, and looked at the horizon. Then, *splash*. The sea turtle surfaced farther out, on the right, sacred reptilian eye blinking open to get a good look at the floating woman scientist.

Olivia said in a timorous voice, "Hi."

And, *plunk*, it was gone. She stared for a long time, but the magnificent creature didn't surface again. She counted the number of wave cycles per second until all sign of the turtle disappeared: *Farewell*. Suddenly all the facts she'd read about sea turtles came flooding into her head. It stored extra oxygen in its body; it could hold its breath for hours.

They'd made it past the chelonian. Khalid pulled her onto sea-worn rock. They climbed to a ledge, then ducked out of the sun and into a cool, dark spot. They were standing in the first cavern in a network of grottos.

Original Love

Animals split from plants 1.547 billion years ago, and humans from animals 14 million years ago. Biocentrics question whether that makes humans the only life form worthy of having rights...

INSIDE THE CHILLY entryway, their eyes took some time to adjust to the dim cavern. When they looked around at last, the first thing they noticed was the smooth stone walls. Sea spray and rising tides had worn away the rock for ages, probably erasing vestiges of any cave paintings there might have been. Olivia had expected that, but still hoped for some kind of clue. For the next hour, they climbed inward. The caves were massive, one leading to another with light pouring in through holes in the ceiling.

Heading toward a speck of light in the darkness, they climbed into a ray of sunlight shining from a meter-wide hole above. The place was fit for primitive life, but they couldn't see any traces of a lost civilization in the chambers. Olivia put her hands on her hips and sighed. "If there was anyone living in these caves, they've been erased for millennia."

"That's good for the sea turtles," Khalid observed.

They swam back in the red afternoon light, searching for the sea turtle in vain. The fish had all gone out to deeper waters. Arms paddled and broke into the free air in tired repetition. Amidst the hush of the waves on the rocks, and hands and feet touching accidentally underwater, disappointment arose. They swam apart. Khalid remained safely distant, as if he knew he had her. Olivia pondered whether he wanted her anymore.

The hill where Khalid had left his yellow backpack grew larger. They climbed out and stumbled along the shore to dry off. Olivia's body tingled. Swimming calibrated everything. She followed Khalid's lead up the rocky escarpment. Khalid picked out a diagonal path, and Olivia followed his footsteps. Small rocks slid down the hill and knocked more rocks onto the beach.

As the heat returned to her limbs, the disappointment of the empty caves got the better of her. "After coming all this way," Olivia said, her upper lip damp and quivering. She climbed after him zigzagging up the green hillside. "I can't believe there's nothing here."

Khalid stopped under a fig tree. His voice was soft and soothing. "Nothing? Legends say there have been four races more advanced than ours living here."

Four! Olivia surveyed the lush slope.

Khalid sniffed the air. "It's wet up here. And the mutation makes roots like a plant, you say?" Khalid said.

"Of course, but."

"Nothing here?" He stood on a ledge and leaned in between two rocks. A thin stream of water trickled down the hill. "There's a spring up here. You'll never have to irrigate this piece of land."

They peered up at the leafy trees gracing the hillside. The sun glowed red on Khalid's back. They penetrated the near jungle-cover of a wild grove. Khalid put his hand on a descendent from a long line of giant trees. "Look at this one. Do you know what it is?" The tree stretched its branches overhead.

Olivia recognized the shape of the leaves Adam and Eve had used to cover their nudity. "Wild Figue vulgaris." This species had fought its way up through natural selection for countless generations. What a coincidence that there were so many figs near the caves.

"The fig hides its secrets, too." Khalid whispered, "(This tree is shy)." He pointed out the green fruit dotting the sky all the way up the ridge to the caves. The network of roots plugged into their source. "These trees know where they came from." The wise creatures communicated through currents underground. If she didn't believe they reached into Earth's dreamy subconscious to shine awareness on the past and channel magnificent complexities through their branches into the light, then how did she explain that the fig had its own species of fig wasp?

"You're so smart."

"There's one, look! Both tree and wasp are dependent on each other to survive," Khalid said. "I tell you, this fig tree is in love. The fig has the hottest sex-life of any plant. Look at this sterile-female flower." He showed Olivia the flower with fig wasp larvae pupating inside. "By late spring, the male wasps direct their energy at the females and fly out with one thought: *love.* They find the virgin female wasps, have sex with them, then die."

"A brief romance," Olivia said, afraid of how much she depended on him, not only for her existence, but now for the key to making the loveoid. Her daymare melded with his train of thought as she pondered the intricacies of wasp courtship.

"Listen to me. I grow figs, and I'm always thinking about love."

She smiled.

"The females fly to the summer syconium and enter again through the small hole where the fig accepts them in order to produce her offspring. They lay hundreds of eggs in the sterile, female flowers and scatter pollen over the fertile ones. They can't inject their eggs into the wrong flowers: see how the flowers that are already fertile are too long? You have all the medicine you need in Nature. *Nobody* has ever loved like a fig tree."

As Khalid explained plant mores, the possibilities for a fig-based loveoid blossomed in Olivia's mind. If figs really did love, there was no need to go around digging in the brains of people who had died while feeling love. What a stroke of luck that would be! She hardly dared to entertain the hope. "There are a few simple experiments we can run to see if it's worth a try."

It was Heaven sent. She inhaled the smell of the sea. And it had always been here. The proximity of the wild fig grove could explain the survival of the race that lived at this site. Despite all his machismo, Khalid actually enabled her to do her research. "Thanks for bringing me here. There's no way I would have discovered the fig trees without you."

"The answer's so well hidden in Nature, no other scientist will ever find it."

"You're impossible," she said, unsure who was whose prisoner.

He took her in his arms. "Olivia. I'm as afraid of you as you are of me."

The ground seemed to disappear beneath her feet. She felt her stomach tugging at her. She hid her face from Khalid.

It was impossible to acknowledge the truth about her backers. Her education, her career, all that money depended on her not recognizing it. They both should be afraid of Big Pharma. "If my backers found out the loveoid came from a tree, they'd try to kill off all the trees."

"What! Why?"

"You can't patent a plant. They'd want to make a derivative of it and make the actual plant extinct." As they climbed, Olivia got the feeling Khalid had guessed more about her funding than he was letting on. The motivation to kidnap her might have already become too strong not to follow through with the act. She glanced at his aquiline features. And he knew she had fallen. His healthy physique. Or worse, if he was innocent. If Big Pharma came looking for its loveoid, she might endanger him as well.

A seagull careened across the path.

"This dirt's very fertile. We'll have to bring some with us." As they climbed higher, Khalid talked about harvesting the olives back home, and about the fruit trees he was going to plant, clementines, apples, and mangos. And about football.

"Did you study agriculture at your university?"

He ignored the question.

Climbing above the wild fig grove, they reached the long, rocky hilltop, the sea on the right, the desert stretching below on the left. Consumed by doubts, Olivia fell silent. One thing had been troubling her for a while now. Khalid had said he'd gone to university in Paris, but later said it was in Portugal. "*Chéri,*" she said, "what university did you say you went to?"

He paused and then said, "I lied, *Bébé*. I didn't go to university. I didn't have the opportunity."

"Oh," Olivia said doubtfully. "That leaves me questioning...," *just about everything: the spending of taxpayers' money, the education system, the sun as God,* "...the meaning of life." Faucheux had once said, "They all lie like they're telling the truth."

Lie upon lie upon lie...upon lay upon lay, precisely what distinguished Khalid from the dead: he created himself, wanted to be other than his Nature, before he sank back into the swamp of the Mother. She looked at her man. Oh well, trust hadn't been one of their fortés to begin with. He seemed to be telling the truth now.

"Is that what they teach at university!"

"They teach what people want to learn. What can you do when there are so many people that there's hardly any wildlife left. Everyone wants to hear how their life is special."

He looked at her questioningly.

"Strictly speaking," she said, "our lives are not special. There are too many humans on the planet. We're lucky if we have a reason to be here."

"We're special to the people around us. So if you want to make a difference, you can appreciate me. Do we need a loveoid for that?"

"We don't, but some do. It'll make some people more loving."

"And that's going to save them from the

mutation?"

"If it works like Zika and other mutations we've been seeing, yes."

They meandered along the rim. The brush had given way to dry clay. They'd come out on a smooth, desert plane. Khalid scanned the plateau. It was so flat, the hilltop seemed to have been shaved off. He started to cross the plateau to see what was on the other side.

Olivia caught up. *Find someone educated,* was the usual advice. But education was precisely the issue. It had come to mean indoctrination. Khalid was unique. Afraid to lose him, and terrified he would destroy her, she let him dig himself out of the lie.

"When I graduated from high school, my parents didn't have any money. I had to work."

"I'm sorry." She grasped at the small consolation that he might be telling the truth now. He needed support. "I'm more impressed that you survived with no university than I would be if you'd gone to a mediocre university. Most 'education' is brainwash anyway." How could society ever make up for training doctors to ignore diet, priests to ignore the body, men to ignore women?

"Brainwash, ha! That's what I thought."

She sighed. "Pretty much." Even the best schools taught students to ignore the population bomb on a finite planet. The higher you rose in the system, the more total the blindness. People believed that growth was sustainable, while the planet wasn't sustaining...

"When I was a boy, I trained with my school's football coach. The national team came to my village for tryouts, and a friend and me, we were picked. My parents said no, I had to study. My friend went on to be a professional player, and got rich. By the time I graduated from high school, my parents didn't have enough money for university, so I had to work in a restaurant on the coast."

As what? she almost asked. She wanted to go back and fix it, at least tell him it was a crying shame. Her throat contracted. "Education is expensive."

"It was a long time ago." He took a step backward. "Why are you crying?"

Olivia blinked her watering eyes.

Khalid swung around, as if he'd felt something behind him.

Then he saw them.

Etched into the desert plateau were countless huge, straight lines of a lighter shade than the ground. *"Tiens."*

They came to the first long straight line carved into the plateau, and had to climb down into the groove and back out again to cross it.

Olivia pointed to the grooves. "Those lines..." She closed her eyes and opened them again. "Holy..."

Khalid bounded toward the nearest etching.

"Who did all that?" She couldn't begin to guess at

any astronomical or calendrical purpose for those crazy lines. "Has anyone else seen these?" She knew the answer just looking at Khalid's face. Only a tiny fraction of history had been recorded. For all man's depletion of natural resources, actual cities only covered three percent of the planet, making it nearly impossible to find the fossils of ancient civilizations.

The lines disappeared into a sand dune. "The sand was blown westward last year by a record-breaking storm," Khalid said.

"I'm sure you can see them from the air. How far is the nearest airport?"

"Three hundred kilometers."

"Those lines must be tens of thousands of years old."

"More."

"Khalid, there's no way man could have made those lines."

Neither could think of any purpose the long scratches might have served. The lines stretched across the perfectly flat plain as if some giant machine had etched them into the clay. The plain resembled a modern runway.

Khalid reached the other side of the plateau first. He was jumping around with his hands on his head.

Olivia ran to the edge. There she saw the strangest thing. Embedded in the rock was an enormous curved drawing so gigantic that you'd never be able to see it from the ground, much less carve it out of the desert: a massive geoglyph of a tortoise.

They were laughing and hugging.

"That turtle looks so friendly." She gazed at the 1200-foot chelonian, bathing in today's sunset. "See how he's sticking his tongue out of the side of his mouth? He's definitely man-made. How could they see what they were doing from down on the ground to carve such a big picture?"

Khalid's arm encircled her waist. "He's welcoming. It looks like a message to whoever landed here and carved those straight lines."

"An invitation to come back. Yes! They were showing someone in space the animal life on Earth."

They teetered on the hilltop, astounded at the animal artists' grit, as if a neighbor from Sol's star-system would hurl back, planets in tow, and want to know where the turtles were.

Khalid and Olivia stood there, amazed, as long as they could, discussing patterns described by the ancients, passed down in lasting masonry and monuments. How much knowledge must be lost. The fragments remaining, secrets shrouded in layers of symbolism, and sand. Then, they sat down to keep on enjoying the view of a piece of the planet's life story. Entranced by the secret the turtle held, Olivia remembered how she'd doubted a team of astronomers, when they found a sibling to Sol, 110 light years away. "They really were on to something." Most stars were born in stellar nursery systems, with matter traveling between solar systems. "The sun came from a cluster of thousands of stars. Sibling stars might have orbited close to Earth in all its five billion years."

Khalid was sure Earth had been seeded by, and seeded, other star systems with life, and could name all twelve of them, "Aries, Taurus, Gemini..."

The sun elongated the shadows on the giant turtle. One thing Olivia and Khalid agreed on, the future of life on Earth would be clear to anyone who observed these carvings. Olivia scooped up a handful of sand and let it flow through her fingers. Whatever was happening to life on the planet now had happened before, and ruling powers knew. There was more to the mystery than her backers cared to solve.

The rustle of a small animal in the brush brought them back to their position in the landscape. They looked up at the deepening sky. Time to head back across the runway.

The trail down was trickier, with avalanches of little rocks sliding more frequently down the embankment into increasing darkness. Khalid paused amidst the figs. He removed his canteen from the backpack. "This land is fertile." He found a jagged rock and scooped dirt into the sack while Olivia took the lead at negotiating the slope.

The waves stopped crashing against the shore. The sea lay in a placid sheet. The blood-red Moon lay engorged beyond the sea-cave peninsula. The

Moon aligned perfectly with the highest peak so its point plunged into, or emanated out of, the heavenly pupil. An orange pyramid of moonlight fanned out across the sea to them.

Olivia raised her arms. "What does it mean?"

"It means we're invited to go swimming again." Khalid scaled down the rest of the slope and took off his sandals.

They waded out. The sea was still warm from the day. Dark water glinted with pieces of the Moon. They plunged. Currents of warm and cold water caressed Olivia's arms as they floated toward the heavenly body; Khalid came swimming after her. She fluttered her feet harder, and swam away. He surfaced, realizing she had eluded him. He sniffed the air, mesmerized by her non-locality, and swam a little faster. Ripples converged. He reached into the alchemical interference pattern and gently grasped her ankle. She gave up on swimming away. He pulled her back. Floating toward him, eyes and nose above the water like a crocodile, she smiled.

Her torso glided alongside his body. Her eyes floated up to his. Starry sky ruled slick sea. She felt his legs curve under hers, and softened into his magnetic grasp. He tilted her into his lap. She floated past, circumambulating his shivering body. She wound her arms around his neck, a tremulous embrace. It wasn't so much the cold, as contagious electricity. She held onto his shoulders. Khalid had one foot under her knees, the other planted in a bed of seaweed.

She slid off and swam. He followed above her back, feet fluttering between her crawl, heading for the Moon.

How Arab Lovers Increase Your Productivity

Plants are among the most vulnerable living beings on the planet. At least one in five plant species is on the brink of extinction, a disastrous loss of biodiversity. Extending 'basic human rights' to plants might mitigate the destruction of the flora, the cornerstone of the natural environment.

A CLOUD OF DUST travelled up the road after a red truck. Olivia came out of the house and waited hands-on-hips in the driveway.

The handymen unloaded three cages of white mice. Olivia opened the door to the tin-roofed shed, and the handymen stacked them on the workbench. She was about to ask them to take a look at the bathroom plumbing when her telephone rang: Khalid.

"Who's that, *Bébé?*"

"The handyman is here to unplug the tub."

"With his boyfriend? Tell them I'll be there in one minute. What do you think they're going to find in there?"

"Probably a cow."

Turned out it was all the plaster Khalid had

dropped in the tub when he was replacing the bathroom tiles.

*

Olivia tagged the mice and set up the experiment. She was excited to get up in the mornings and started to call them by name.

In the afternoons, she helped tend Khalid's figs with extra care. The sturdy trees flourished. Wasps buzzed around the fruit ripening in the sun. Khalid and Olivia harvested the purple fruit, and extracted ingredients for the loveoid from the seeds. Weeks of experimentation lapsed into a month.

Their tomatoes, broccoli, peppers, barley and cabbage also miraculously grew despite brackish water. Olivia softened towards Khalid. He was being much nicer and certainly more authentic than any of Faucheux's team. Always on his own, communing with Nature, his identity was in terms of his place in the ecosystem, no matter the consequences. When he expressed his feelings, his body looked so happy and healthy.

Khalid was easier to work with these days. He approached chemistry like a cook, and could actually sniff out changes of enzymatic state. His exceptional 'nose' could have earned him a comfortable living at a French perfume maker, had he been allowed in the country. Olivia grew accustomed to him watching over her shoulder in the lab, and postulating during breaks. She knew he valued her love, and came to understand why he held his political point of view.

One morning, she opened the shed and found one test tube with a different color than the rest. Could it be? Working in the calm, Olivia was able to isolate an endorphin that seemed to connect strong emotional feelings with altruism, the beginnings of love. She ran tests against the virus sample taken from the mayor's aerial root.

"How's it going?" Khalid asked, standing in the doorway.

"I just have to find a way to get the endorphin to release oxytocin in the mice." But the isolated pieces proved more Delphic than expected. Turning the problem over, she reviewed the process for the 300th time, trying to fit the puzzle back together. Several days later, the mice still showed no change. "I can't work here. This setup is too…simple."

"We have to break your American mold. You're seeing the problem from the wrong angle. You're trying to master the parts. Become part of the whole, like me."

"I'm fine. The problem is this lab."

"Don't complain. You will be without the present for the rest of eternity."

"Come on, this workbench is too small."

"If you insist." He took the test tube from her and

swirled it, smelled it, and wrinkled his nose. He planted it in his mental womb. "The flavor is off."

"You're not going to drink it!"

"I'm telling you, if you're going to be negative, at least be right. Smells and flavors are chemically the same. Your company has you thinking like a machine. They want to turn people into robots. Their approach is simply backwards." He warned her not to let the process run itself. You had to de-automatize. Get in the flow. Then the whole experiment would become a meditation and link to the divine.

"We're not going to leave it up to chance."

"There's no such thing. Chance is when you don't perceive the cause. You might be brilliant theoretically, but if you want to isolate love, you have to be involved. At least keep the kitchen clean — why would your Cupid want to come around here? There's no flow to your work space." Khalid started to push test tubes, gardening tools, the yellow backpack full of dirt, the relic — no, that he put on a top shelf — the mouse cage, to the edge of the workspace. In a frenzy, he cleaned the countertop with a rag.

"OK, OK!" Olivia finished cleaning up. Khalid had convinced her. Nothing else had worked. Serendipity might be the only hope. She tried to keep alert but at the same time lose herself in the zone. He assisted, as Olivia re-made the solution.

She kept moving, going with the flow. Her body became agile, functioning in unity with existence. Maybe the divine would visit her mindful repetition. "Let's pray."

"That's better." The work piqued Khalid's need to probe beneath the obvious for the hidden order of things. Determined to pull out the truth, he took the new solution from her and held it over the Bunsen burner.

"It's not supposed to be heated!"

"Did it say that on the package?" He was tired of losing. He held the tube with a hot pad and swirled it above the flame. "You have to make a circle with it for a long time."

"Why's that?"

"The circle is an expanded point. It symbolizes the spirit and the cosmos."

"OK."

"It's a secret, but I'm going to show you anyway." His eyes twinkled. "The circle is made up of some thing (the unbroken line), and no thing (the space inside and outside the line). That's how the circle unifies spirit and matter."

The mice ventured from the corner of their cage to watch.

"You have to mix it with love." Khalid sucked up the mixture with a dropper. He stuck his gloved hand into the cage and scooped up a fat white mouse. He held it firmly against his chest. "Here you go, Shaaban."

The mouse swallowed the liquid.

Khalid stroked him and put him back in his cage with his mate.

Olivia fell asleep reassured. Waiting to see if Khalid's brainchild would work, they enjoyed a pastoral week farming and cooking, with Khalid playing music till late.

The next week, the mice still showed no changes. Olivia put the mice back into their cage. "I can't believe it."

"We've tried everything. This is crazy. Why do we need a loveoid? We have love."

"It's my work. Why don't you stop farming? Let's go to a restaurant."

This shook things up. Khalid ignited with unpredictable volatility. His fist came down on a loose plank. "We will NOT go to a restaurant!" The mouse food and the bag of dirt slid off the work table, hit a shovel and spilled on the floor.

"Now look what you did!" Olivia said, but he was gone.

And it was her job to fix everything...*good reason to live, humiliating women.* The red dirt from the caves had landed all over the mouse food. She got a dustpan and broom and tried to remove the red Earth from the brown food, *impossible.* In the end, she had to let the mice sort it out. She gave them enough water and food mixture for a week, swept the rest into a box and stowed it on the Earth floor under the worktable. *At least the place is clean.*

*

Olivia resettled on the terrace. She listened to Khalid's wandering notes from the field and contemplated the direction stupidity was taking life on Earth. Suicide for the human race, and homicide for so many species. The hunting of the most loving by the lowest. It was ubiquitous. Viscous feral cats killed the most refined ones; government terrorists assassinated the Martin Luther Kings.

When Olivia finally did go back into the lab, she found Shaaban cuddled right up to his female, who was very chubby. *Pregnant?* She took urine, saliva and blood samples.

The lab took on a whole new aspect. A sanctity had descended, even on the gardening tools. The results were positive. Olivia ran to find Khalid, and led him back to the lab. A contagious grin spread across her face. She hugged him. Her euphoria had an alchemical effect on him. He twirled her around. They were on the path. The loveoid was in sight.

They calmed down and went into the kitchen for a brief celebration over a cup of coffee. It was a beginning. There was a lot of work ahead. Seriousness set in. It wouldn't be easy. Too bad for the ones already rooted to the ground; there would never be any way to reverse the damage for those who'd already mutated.

"At least they make oxygen," Khalid said. "That's more than before."

"At least we can still save the rest."

"'Keep it clean and it will heal itself,'" Khalid said.

"I figure out how to stop the mutations, and — "

"A year ago, we had bad people on top. Now the water's clean. Why does it always have to be black or white? Leave the clouds. Choose in the rainbow."

Olivia wavered. The other extreme could be dangerous as well. "You think the ones left are fit to run things just because they're in love?" Yet, he had a point: maybe the loveoid wasn't the path to truth.

"Maybe the truth *is* love."

"I need to run the experiment again with another couple of mice."

"Again!"

With renewed energy, Olivia opened a new bag of clean food, and set the experiment up again properly...

...with no results.

Her arms slumped forward. She avoided Khalid's gaze. Nothing worked here. She was at a loss, trying to figure this out, and turned her back on him. About to leave the shed, she placed her foot on the threshold, then stopped short.

In that instant, looking wide-eyed at the courtyard, Olivia felt Khalid's labyrinthine mystique come into sharp focus. She felt her mind reeling back through her entire career, her tiny self trapped in a corner of the maze. Next, her research since leaving the Institute looped in a tight circuit. Everything she and Khalid had experienced fell into place. In the sky, light outlined the clouds, and highlighted the obstacles. Mind racing as she pieced together the puzzle, her focus shifted to the deep blue way out.

Khalid was already hunting around in the corner of the shed. "I told you."

"You did not!"

Six Things Your Boss Might Expect You to Know about Arab Lovers

The new big foodie enthusiasm? Earthy recipes from the very soil that nourishes life. Le Plat Sal, a gastronomic restaurant in the Marais of Paris, prepares signature dishes alive with vitamin- and mineral-rich Earth, such as Boue Ragout, a mud stew.

THEY FOUND THE DIRT MIXTURE. Khalid dropped a handful on the workbench. "It was the dirt."

"I can't believe it." Olivia re-ran the experiment with the food-dirt mixture...

Eureka! The soothsayer's phrase came back to Olivia. *What you seek is in the last place you look.* The most counterintuitive thing imaginable. "After centuries of Christianity's, 'Cleanliness is next to godliness'."

"As is darkness next to light." In the kitchen, Khalid was baking the dirt at 80 degrees for two hours to kill any parasites. "Wait till the world finds out!"

This would turn the pharmaceutical industry upside down. "I don't think it wants to know. You can't patent dirt."

"You can't drive dirt to extinction, either. Ha! It's

over. I should have seen it before. 'Salt' was an ancient name for dirt. Now your Big Pharma will never, ever, ever make back its investment." He looked quite smug.

A toothy grin spread across Olivia's face. What a wonderful revelation! A dark secret in plain daylight. *Earth is rich in minerals.* "An excellent preventative treatment."

"Bien sur." Khalid started laughing. "Dirt is what the mutant's roots were seeking! *Imaginez* pharmaceuticals trying to patent dirt."

The idiocy was contagious. It infected Olivia. She held onto her stomach, doubling over. "Haaaaah, cooking with dirt!" Inanity bubbled, melting boundaries until their thoughts evaporated, and they forgot what they were laughing about. Olivia let her phone ring. The sound of Khalid's spasmodic boom and her high-pitched tinkling caused deeper, more genuine laughing.

Olivia's phone rang on. "Drop it," Khalid said through the last convulsions.

Taking advantage of his good humor, Olivia picked it up anyway.

Or maybe not. Khalid stood up, knocking his chair over. A manager from the facility yelled about deadlines over the phone. Olivia thought about the seven billion. Nine zeros had a leveling effect. It cost four billion to develop and get a medicine through government regulations for testing on people. Of that four billion, only ten million was supposed to be her cut. Still, seven zeros was plenty.

She could do good work with the money...but enough to counter the destruction wreaked by saving those in power with the loveoid? If Khalid knew about even one million, he'd never let her go.

*

Her phone rang daily now. "When are you going to deliver the loveoid? We need to know what stage it's in."

Someone barked a question in the background. A Faucheux type. She got the unpleasant taste in her mouth that she always got when she was around him. She was glad she'd escaped that culture. Faucheux probably died in the hotel lobby attack. Or if not, he would have been a good candidate for the mutation. She was certain she couldn't have convinced him to eat dirt, however much she would have liked to.

Olivia steadied her voice. "Since the loveoid is still in its initial stages, it's unstable. Transporting it by air would upset its effectiveness," she said, pacing up and down. "It needs at least a few more weeks before it's ready for federal testing." When she turned around, she stood face-to-face with Khalid. The phone fell from her hand.

"Who's that?" Khalid demanded, knowing full

well who it was.

"Work," Olivia whispered.

"How can you justify working for those thieves? A loveoid isn't love."

"Correct. It's love-like," she whispered, picking up her phone. She switched it off.

Khalid grabbed her arms. "You think they're paying you so much money for your discovery. Why would they? It would be better if they were paying you less. Then it wouldn't be worth it to have you killed."

Her voice slid up an octave. "Let them try," she said. "There are too many people anyway. The planet is beyond carrying capacity."

"And farmers are killing themselves." He pulled her closer. "How much are they paying you?"

She wriggled away.

"You think everybody wants to steal from you. Be careful. I tell you, I know more about fighting than they do."

"Great, maybe you can save me again."

He yelled in her ear. "I can't save you. You have to save yourself!"

Olivia choked on her saliva. She felt the heat rise to her face.

"You know they're wrong, and you don't take action. I'll show you how much I understand." He folded his arms. "Until you break that brainwashed mold, I'll treat you as the slave you're acting like."

How *could* you justify seven billion octane? She had to keep Khalid out of it.

But Khalid was already soaking the dirt to extract the mineral salts.

An hour later, Olivia heard him emptying leftovers into Wahad's dish, a good time to disappear for a while. She mulled the situation over as she walked through the orchard. She always thought better around trees. The vibe calmed among crisscrossed branches, and roots extending deep into the Earth. Her life seemed slightly less out of control. She just had to get a grip. How could she keep Khalid out of the loveoid? She needed to find his Achilles' heel.

For all his bravery, Khalid was afraid of scandal. Olivia still couldn't work out whether he had secret plans for her or was just deeply shy. Coming back from her walk, she crossed the courtyard and opened the door to her laboratory. She stood back, aghast.

Waxing Sun

The most significant difference between plants and humans is that plants have a specialized cellular structure called chloroplasts enabling them to derive energy from sunlight through photosynthesis. Thus, plants are capable of making their own food, while chloroplastless humans depend on other living things for survival.

ALL HER TEST TUBES lay smashed on the floor. Shards of glass littered the workbench. The loveoid was splattered on every surface.

She reeled, and held onto the doorknob. What a disaster. She would never be able to get back to zero.

She found Khalid in the field. He was scraping red dirt from potatoes and chucking them into a bushel. He didn't look up or say anything.

She shook her fists in his face. "You betrayed me! You said you'd help me make the loveoid."

"Dirt works better. Your chemical isn't safe."

"I still have to deliver a chemical! Why did you wreck the lab?"

"You think you're better than me."

"I do not! There's that chip on your shoulder. Is that your self-education?" Olivia's voice cracked. "Power isn't degrading others. It inspires. I never said I was better. What an idea! That is *too bad.*"

He hung his head. Broad shoulders just a lump.

She wanted to pound his shoulders with her fists. Instead, tears streamed down her face. So much of their relationship had been a reaction to old wounds. They looked daggers at each other, unable to hide what the other found unattractive.

Olivia wiped her nose on her sleeve. She squatted down next to him. "That's no excuse for destroying the loveoid! I think you're at least as smart as I am. Do you understand?"

He broke a twig and threw the pieces on the ground. "Well, you said—"

His voice was drowned out by a steady beating like the wings of a very large bird. The sound grew louder. They squinted into the sun. A helicopter flew over the hill. It was closing in on the farm. Olivia jumped up. "They're coming for me."

Khalid raised his fist to the sky.

"Why do they hate women?" Olivia screamed, running for the house.

"Because they're becoming women!" Khalid yelled.

The copter chopped overhead. Its shadow engulfed Olivia. A loudspeaker blared from a tornado of wind. "Close in. Easy."

Two armed henchmen leapt from the chopper. One ran straight to the shed. He rushed in and came right back out yelling.

The pilot maneuvered the copter in a tremendous

torrent of wind and noise, as the other henchman chased down Olivia. A tether dropped from the copter. It hit her on the back. She lost her footing and fell to the ground. "Khalid!"

Before Khalid could run back to help, the other henchman tackled him. They rolled in the dust, hands on each other's necks.

"Khalid!" Olivia screamed.

The henchman left her lover lying there, body still.

The killer was coming for her. She ran as fast as she could, but he ran faster. He caught Olivia around the middle and tethered her to the copter.

The henchmen jumped into the open doorway. The bird ascended, lifting Olivia off the farmland chessboard, and toting her into the sky.

Incarceration

*With the world catapulted into another medieval crusade,
we are reminded that the West has on numerous occasions
blown itself up with its own bombs, and pointed the finger
at others.*

THE HELICOPTER flew out of a cloud of dust. The
first thing Olivia noticed was the enormous
greenhouse in the middle of the facility where an
atrium must have been. The helicopter hovered over
the roof. Two guards untethered her. The beating of
the wings came to a halt. The pilot descended. "It
wasn't easy rescuing you."

Olivia sized up the handcuffs dangling from his
belt. She'd had time to think. She slowed her
breathing. "Thank you. Sorry if I seem shocked. It's
been a traumatic experience."

"I'll bet."

They made their way downstairs. "Left," he said.
He led her through a hallway with many offices.
Blue track lighting shone on the furniture and
abstract paintings adorned the walls in a series of
lounge areas. "Over there." She turned at the plant
with rocks in its pot. They walked down a hallway
with many doors. They stopped at the second one on

the left. "Now here's a place where you can really concentrate." And with that, he dropped her off at her room.

Olivia surveyed the ground-floor ensuite. It had a view of the city on one side, and a terrace with a view of the sea on the other. There were clothes in the closet — lab attire, a Pacco Luigi evening gown with the $19,979 price tag on it, and a Brazilian cut bikini from Doll in a Box. In the fridge were grapes, Camembert, a vegetarian dinner, and a bottle of wine. In the next room, the state-of-the-art lab she'd had in mind. It was fully equipped with a constant-sample-temperature, strong-deceleration centrifuge; a comprehensive rack of chemicals; an electron microscope — upwards of a million dollars... They'd even supplied a Vestiges briefcase, $8739. Everything but love.

Khalid! What she wouldn't give to be back in the makeshift lab with him. She crumbled onto the bed and cried.

There was a knock at the door. She wiped her face.

A taxi driver waited, patiently holding a cage of mice. She tried to get his telephone number, but he pretended not to understand her. She noticed the armed sentries posted at the end of the hallway and in the garden. Her 'rescuers' had no intention of letting her go until she produced. She was left to set up her experiments.

Wave Masquerade

As the planet warms, evolutionary changes are surfacing in most species, modifying our DNA, hormones, minds, perhaps enabling us to surf gravitational waves into other dimensions.

A CAR PASSED with the windows rolled down, radio on loud. The oversized facility slumbered in darkness, except for a flame peering from one window. Through it, wafted a string of eighth notes insensible as nails hitting a tin can, the muse for a guarded experiment even less logical.

When she awoke at five a.m., the dusty street was bare, except for a bar dancer, who took off her four-inch heels and scurried through the parking lot. Olivia peeked out the beach window. Another misty morning. No horizon line to calibrate sea and sky today. Heaven and Earth were one: anything was possible.

She didn't believe in air-conditioning and preferred to work in the cool of half-light. The sun mounted. It burnt off the humidity. Olivia moved the test tubes into the coolest corner of the room. She blockaded the windows to preserve her trials and errors. In the late afternoon it was finally cool enough to open the shutters. The town wound inward toward entanglement.

She'd heard Axel survived the attack. Maybe he could help... What a change that would be. When she wasn't praying for Khalid's soul, she drudged night and day to re-engineer a chemical-based loveoid that mimicked the properties of dirt...a version of the loveoid that might buy her freedom.

The mist rolled in. Another trial. The marble floor sweat with humidity. Early morning noises threw off sleep. She puttered about in the purple dawn. Her mice showed no change. The evening sun bowed beneath the palms. For all the chemicals and high-tech processing, the only pill she was able to come up with performed worse than even the fig-based loveoid. The best prevention was the dirt. An actual cure was nowhere in sight.

The days grew cooler, with dry wind from Egypt, where demonstrations waged on. You could move around without sweating, and go outside at noon. She was working just to get to zero. *Khalid was right*.

She grieved for her former captor. She ached for his funny way of loving. *Allah, please protect Khalid. Take care of him better than you did in life.*

Hang-up

The debate over whether plants have minds, souls, and rights is being waged in halls of justice.

THROUGH SHEER COMPLIANCE, Olivia gained the confidence of her hosts.

Her supervisor, a timid, introverted woman a few years older, looked up from a report on the most recent transplant. A mutant from Trident Fuel in New York.

"The Trident case! How did it happen?" Olivia asked.

"It says his secretary found him. He'd had the usual symptoms of incessant and repetitive language, change of pigmentation."

"Is that a first-hand account of his last days?" How she'd love to see that!

"Yes. It says the secretary witnessed his decline. The usual digressions became more noticeable while handling business decisions — "

"...promoting dirty energy," Olivia said.

"Well. Then, he slipped into the excessive verbiage. After three weeks, she came in and found him fully mutated and unable to speak. When she went around his desk, he was stuck to the carpet."

In search of Earth. "So that's how it happens. The virus affected proteins that switched his latent plant genes on. Earth reclaimed him, and he went back to his pre-mammalian roots."

"So it seems," the director said. Whatever had been triggered in his DNA to revert him to planthood enabled the production of chloroplast.

"Now he's sustainable, making his own food, the way our plant ancestors have done for hundreds of millions of years." Olivia folded her arms. "Wouldn't he rather be in his home country?"

Olivia's director slid the report across the counter. "Taking care of these guys here is expensive, but euthanizing them requires laws we don't have. Add to that the complication that the mutants aren't capable of speech."

Olivia was thrilled to open the report.

Her director put her pen in her pocket. "At the meetings, they act like they might abandon them to a woods." The Assembly Health Committee had approved a bill that allowed terminal patients to end their lives, however, abandoning an individual who was not in the actual throes of death, was illegal.

"It's natural to echo free will," Olivia said. *And even more natural to do what they're told.*

Although the center was overflowing with these gentle creatures, it would have to make room for one more.

Olivia tried not to look surprised when she was

handed an envelope containing a code-red security pass. She felt a surge of adrenaline. The pass would give her access to the Grand Arboretum.

None of the other scientists had seen it. None had wanted to, for fear of contagion. Olivia took the envelope down to the high-security atrium.

The entrance was marked with red-and-white-striped security tape. The guard stepped aside. *Finally, the Grand Arboretum.* A peaceful forest scent welcomed her. Except for a TV, a gardener and a cleaning woman, Olivia was alone. It didn't feel that way, though. Perhaps it was the humidity. She studied the branches extending to vaulting ceilings. She listened for signs of consciousness.

She'd never expected an investment this huge to build a structure for people beyond hope. Was this going on everywhere? The financing should be reallocated to prevent the mutation from hitting the rest. The logical thing to do was to inform the public about the live anti-virals and nutrients in plain old Earth. While remaining within the four walls of her medical indoctrination. An impossible task.

There was enormous resistance. Her degree was so admired back on the East Coast. She'd gone along with the hoopla while she was growing up there — this kind of problem would have inspired her back then. Before she learned biochemical dogma: the bio was the human, and the chemical was the medicine. That division was enforced with warfare. The creed dictated that only a small percentage of the human genome was shared with plants. It completely ignored new research forcing that percentage upward all the time.

Science refused to see. It took awhile for you to notice it. And once you were aware, no one understood. Blind science ruled out biological cures. Anything you couldn't patent wasn't worth the investment. The pressure to conform was inconceivable. Yesterday an intern had sabotaged another team's food experiment. The doctors went along with the prank, trying their hardest to climb to the next rung themselves. Sheer insanity.

No one could mimic dirt chemically. No one should want to.

Such was the situation that November afternoon when she stood under the foliage in the Grand Arboretum for the first time. If you looked closely, you could still see faces on some of the plants.

A newly planted tree laureated the entryway. Knots dilated where the eyes had been. She stood face-to-face with the former CEO of Trident Fuel, and recognized the utter pointlessness of her job. His clownish chin now extended into an elegant branch with tiny leaves. His legs had disappeared in the tethering to Mother Earth. She touched the trunk, solid wood, no reaction. You couldn't save them from themselves. She checked vital signs, kicked his root, *firm*, and moved on.

Her hands swiftly plucked dead leaves off trees. Some of them were bearing fruit, proof you could go on to lead a productive life after mutation.

When she came to the third patient, she flipped through her clipboard in shock: an oligarch, a sheik, and the oil CEO. The first three advanced-stage victims were top brass. All known for their greed. The mutation really did start with the most machinelike, greedy egomaniacs; people who used people, and loved things.

The expressions on the trees looked relieved. It was as if they needed to urgently reconnect with the planet...*root of the word 'plant'*...and the body's response was to sprout an urgent lifeline. Nature compensated by forcing them to connect, forcing them to love. The common denominator of the many different kinds of love was connection...*an epiphany in every sense.*

At first they grew aerial roots like orchids, to suck moisture out of the air, *and then these.* She felt the root of a fully converted banker. The wooden cord was as wide as her hand. She read the name on his tag. A well known *financière.*

She hurried around the greenhouse reading the tags. Some of their charts had news clippings. The nerve! She could only think of one thing these head honchos might have in common biochemically: a long chain of deficiencies starting with oxytocin — in lay terms, a loss of empathy for their fellow beings.

Flipping through her notes, Olivia's hands trembled. The pen dropped and stuck in the dirt. Nature really had made a U-turn. She was hunting down the predators. An answer to her prayers. She could hardly believe the about-face.

Olivia finished inspecting the trees. Every last one of the advanced-stage victims brought here for a cure was a wealthy business oligarch. Major confirmation. Her funding was all to save rulers-turned-epiphyte from the top of elaborate hierarchies. *Khalid was right.* These were predators whose machinations were so sinister, they were no longer human. She didn't want to think what crimes had evoked justice.

It made sense. The area was high security to keep the privileged status of the patients a secret. It was just wrong. By moral standards, these patients had brought the world to this impasse. Even as trees, they continued to take more than their share.

The TV screen on the wall near the exit showed taxis and buses abandoned amidst vines and foliage. The news flash panned over parks sprouting helter-skelter on Madison Avenue in New York, former icon of modernity. Trees rooted to potholes in the middle of streets could not be cut down. The city where euthanasia was still illegal had some soul searching to do.

Work was being reorganized according to

location. You simply had to grow your own food to survive. Vegans were the majority now. Many more had been forced to discover dry fasting. They'd slowed their metabolisms to such a point of efficiency that they needed almost no food to live. A Danish woman was interviewed, "Hardly a tragedy if you consider how obese humans have become and how many other species we've been killing off that are now making a comeback." The camera panned along with a line of ducklings following their mother down Åboulevard in Copenhagen. New populations of birds immigrated into cities, further challenging those who had escaped dehumanization and its flip side, natural rejection.

Tea Bag

Tyrants, however powerful, ultimately suffer by poisoning their own souls.

OLIVIA BURST through the doors.

The security guard tightened his grip on his baton, then nodded to her.

A team of researchers standing around the coffee machine straightened up. She sensed their anxiety, and started to slip away, but the extrovert of the group stopped her in her tracks. "Dr. Murchadha! We were asked to read your paper."

Olivia held her clipboard to her chest. She recognized Santiago, a survivor from Hôtel Dido.

"We just wanted to know, does the virus fit into your love theory?" Santi had just started working on Axel's experiment the day before the attack. "You classify love as a survival instinct. Why would the rule wear thin in our era?"

Because it doesn't. Khalid was right about so many things. Truth was hidden in plain sight. Who knew if the rule held from the lowest microbe *all the way* up? What was the highest being on the spectrum, anyway? Some form of energy only separated from Unity by a thin veil of aether? Did higher life forms cannibalize each other, too? Could we change? Would evolution in the human race tip the natural order? Had Axel evolved?

They were all staring at her.

"Good question."

A colleague in mismatched socks blocked the coffee machine. "That's like asking why there's Zika now."

Olivia reached for a chamomile tea bag, and pointed it toward the hot water. Parting her colleagues, she filled her cup. "Why now? Evolution's been disrupted. Our eco-disaster's instigated a number of game changers. The enormous amount of prehistoric ice that's melting at both poles is enough to unleash an array of undreamed-of microbes. We'll be lucky if only one new-old virus triggers mutations."

"An increase in mutations does seem likely," Santiago agreed.

Olivia took notice of him...a doctor who wasn't indoctrinated. *How did he get in?*

A frustrated colleague challenged him, but Santiago stood his ground. "It's proven." Some vertebrates gave birth in the wild by asexual reproduction. An increase in virgin births had been recorded among Komodo dragons, snakes, birds, and sharks. Rare and endangered species colonizing new habitats were the most likely candidates for parthenogenesis. Florida's endangered small-toothed sawfish was a case-in-point. It started with an egg dividing, breaking off a sister cell with the same set of chromosomes, then the sister cell reconnected with the egg, fertilizing it like sperm.

The discussion proceeded with pre-ordained circularity. "Mutation in plants and animals is one thing," said the colleague with one orange and one brown sock, "but to imply that man's one of the animals that changes sexes to fill environmental need!"

Olivia took a deep breath and went there. "First of all, there's more than one divide among the sexes. On the love scale, we're dealing with movable parts. The ancients were ahead of us. Navajo Indians recognized four genders: man, woman, masculine female-bodied, and feminine male-bodied. It's probable that the most masculine men on the spectrum can only find the path to Eros with a small fraction of the most feminine women. Where does that leave love?"

"We also didn't agree with your linking overpopulation to a rise in homosexuality," said a willowy scientist.

"Well, it would champion homosexuals as a cure for overpopulation, but why get hung up on sex? The more interesting issue is love. For man to use people and worship things is robotic. No surprise that Nature would force him to reconnect with his roots."

"You say 'his'."

"When they bring in a female case, I'll add 'her'." Of course, there were plenty of female cases, just none at the tip-top who were getting the red-carpet treatment.

The scientists exchanged glances. One muttered, "Love as a survival skill! No wonder the Institute wasn't thrilled."

"The Institute is just the pawn of the Consortium," said Santiago.

Olivia froze. "The Consortium?" *There's more than one funder?*

Santiago flipped to the bottom of the pile of papers on his clipboard to a page with twenty logos underneath. Olivia stared at all the companies backing her research. She pressed her lips together. The same companies on the tags in the greenhouse. She watched him turn the page and drew in her breath. Faucheux's name. Ugh. He was alive. And next to it, *designated local contact point.*

Of all people! They had to pick one who was only interested in using his position to squash others. Olivia felt sorry for all the researchers he'd driven to depression. She couldn't believe she was still working for him. He was unfit for the task of life. She shuddered to think what kind of beasts lurked above Faucheux, all the thought leaders they'd assassinated for various sacrileges, essentially against economic growth. Kennedy, countless environmentalists, the guru Osho — that one erased freedom of religion from *The Constitution*.

Her lab coat was suddenly too hot. She juggled her clipboard and phone and took it off. Forcing her stomach out into a ball to inhale more deeply, she tried to calm the thought parade in her mind. Statistically speaking, Faucheux's game should already have stopped working. A multitude of research had shown that givers thrived more than takers in the long run. It was turning her stomach. Just the thought of feeding Faucheux's power games so he could humiliate others. It was too much. After all her efforts, she'd come full circle. If being a bloodsucker meant professional success, she had to step off the treadmill.

Santiago followed her. "Obviously, if shrimp can sense an overabundance of males and switch sexes, not to mention hormone disrupters like atrazine..."

He knew his sexology, alright, but was still no match for Axel's erudition. "Listen, could you deliver a message to one of our colleagues at the Dido facility?"

The new UK Prime Minister, Leicester Davies, held a press conference in which he labelled the mutations the "worst health crisis in human history". A state of emergency has been declared in several countries including New York, France, the UK and Germany.

AN EGG-SHAPED EUTHANASIA candidate made his way through the breakfast room with a glass of sparkling wine. After giving up on life, daybreak with alcohol would be one of the final consolations. The sight of him reminded Olivia to go back to the salad bar for a hard-boiled egg to have *à la maison*. She stashed it in her pocket and put her tray on the conveyor belt. She had work to do. But her only idea was to play along until an opportunity for escape arose.

Olivia headed back to her suite. She checked the control group of mice. They were dirt-fed for comparison to those fed with the chemical loveoid. She observed the control group snuggled up together in the corner of their cage. They appeared considerably more altruistic, and were making high levels of oxytocin after only three days of eating dirt. She noted how their eyes sparkled. Even their conjunctivitis had cleared up.

Peeling the egg, she looked in the mirror at her hair, frizzy from the humidity, at her white skin, the bags under her eyes. She'd slaved herself into a frenzy for Faucheux. She couldn't work on the useless loveoid anymore. She took the control group cage out to the grass and let the mice go.

What would happen if she tried to go swimming in the sea? Would they carry her back here? She wondered how far she could get. She had to know. Her pearl earrings seemed too big, and she didn't have any flip-flops, but she'd have to make do. She covered herself in fifty-SPF sunscreen, tucked a few coins in her bikini top, and pulled on her sundress.

Heads turned to look at her as she walked by the pool. *"Ooo, Bébé."* The suitors weren't more than eighteen years old, maybe farmers, like Khalid. *God protect my bronze man.*

The sun shone through the palm leaves. It diffracted into a mandala of color.

She meowed at a cat still nestled from the night in the crotch of a tree. There were no guards in sight. The infinite blue sparkled to the steady rhythm of waves lapping at the shore.

She hurried down the path. The cement burned her feet. She ran down to the water and took off her dress. Then she heard a man's voice calling. *"Fata! Fata!"* A guard in a long-sleeve black shirt and long pants was running toward her.

They'd given her the swim suit. Was she

supposed to swim in the pool? A cool wave covered her foot, sea shining in anticipation. The guard's uniform was no match for her bikini.

"*Fata!*" It had been awhile since she'd been called a girl. She wasn't going to disappoint him by turning around.

Olivia dove in and swam as fast as she could. She kicked up a crest and pretended not to hear him, standing on the shore yelling.

Normally, she didn't swim out this far. She told herself she was a good swimmer. She just had to make it to the tourist area.

Morning light penetrated the low-amplitude waves. Now there was only the sea. Its caress, the saline balm of forgiveness. She had never noticed the starbursts playing on the water before. Messengers that governed all the laws of Nature, slowing down to the speed of light, from an invisible field of consciousness beyond space and time. These bursts of energy on the placid waves flashed their awareness like so many cameras. Their vibrations beyond the world of matter. Her body became more agile, rippling through an infinite sea of potentials. As she beheld this energy, she connected to an infinite field where all possibilities existed. There was nothing to believe; she could see it with her own eyes. The waves went on glinting from their dimension made up of light, frequency, energy, vibration, information, consciousness. Filling her with knowing. Invisible waves of energy from some quantum multiverse, available for her to use in the creation of her future.

Fish rippled beneath the surface. Sand-colored bodies patterned the turquoise. Flutter kicking underwater, Olivia floated along the shore speckled with white umbrellas and bronze bathers. No showing off here; the very few women were covered in burkas. *Jealousy afoot.* The white facades of the buildings in the sunlight all looked the same. She glided along, trying to figure out which one was Hôtel Dido...

She had gone quite a distance without anyone stopping her. Victory. A self-organizing awareness had observed all of the universes and galaxies into order; it would keep a divine eye out for her, too. She had to get out and look around, come up with a plan.

The clear salt water rippled, alive with little black fish. A baby Solea vulgarilis wriggled underfoot. Another slab of sand on the bottom disengaged. A flounder gave up its camouflage. Even if she was still being followed, this mixture of bikinis and other swimmers in billowing scarves lightened her mood. The lengths they'd go to.

She stepped onto the beach and spotted a poolside bar. A friendly local took her order with a smile. Another wiped the counter. She took her mango smoothie to a divan. The heat melted her will, and soon she drifted into slumber.

"Mommy!" A child somewhere. Her eyes opened a slit: blue sky and a sprig of orderly pine needles. No one in sight. She sat up. A black yacht at eye-level careened up to the dock. It freed its sun-saturated crew.

The heat became overbearing, and she realized she was the only one out under the open sky. Saltwater foam bubbled along the shore. The zenith air was rife with static electricity. She had the feeling she was being watched.

A visual feast of cacti lined the sea path. Olivia halted and turned on the beach shower. She got under it.

Completely cooled down now, she continued along and forgot about her body. Windsurfers were coming out, lime-green stripes gliding on the azure, and what was that beyond the hibiscus? She could have sworn she saw someone move. The yacht had departed and was sailing along the horizon line. A breeze rustled the leaves.

There was the sign she hadn't seen from the sea, *Hôtel Dido, End It All.* The palms swayed in the soft breeze. She wanted to run to Axel for help. But faced with the actual hotel, she worried she was being unrealistic. Axel had a strong tendency toward conditional action. He might refuse without something in exchange.

There was only one person by the pool, an old

woman who'd fallen asleep in the sun. Where was the old misogynist when you needed him? What a scandal that would be, searching the lobby for Axel in her bikini.

She sat on a bench. The plan was to drift in the unknown until the universe gave the signal. Turning slightly, she noticed a man walking at a distance behind her. He slowed his gait and shot her a flagrant stare. A chill ran down her spine. He came to a full stop in front of her and peered into her face with half-closed eyes. Nausea engulfed her.

But the intruder spoke with the voice of a woman. "Miss," the person said with desert-meets-sea urgency. "Excuse me, Miss. My *rayiys* asked me to hire you."

A wave of relief: at least Olivia still owned her sexual provender. She made no response, easing into the gray area.

"If you would like to earn one hundred, he would be delighted to pass the evening in your hotel room."

How disgusting. But the stranger's politesse calmed Olivia's fears. She could just see the fat old *rayiys* eating from his knife, sitting in the sun with his mouth open like a crocodile, pretending to get along with the rest of her mice.... What would her keepers think?

Sensing her hesitation, the go-between became more boisterous.

A surge of adrenaline slowed Olivia's breathing. *Every decision necessarily shuts down every other decision.* She lingered in indecisiveness, buying time. "So good of you to ask." And found herself vying to keep her options open. "My husband and I have never met him."

The intruder took her arm. "One hundred and fifty."

"Please give your boss my apologies. My husband is expecting me," Olivia lied.

The woman twisted Olivia's arm and brought her to her feet. "Let's be clear," she sneered. "I know who you work for, and I know why."

Trapped. If Olivia could stay in the gray area long enough to create a way out... The spy twisted harder. Of course, there would be other groups interested in the loveoid. There would be predators everywhere she went.

"Terrible things are behind us. We are done atoning for the deeds of the men you cure. Evil is punished."

Olivia thought fast. "My captors have already proven their unworthiness by hurting my husband. How do I know you would be any better?"

"Powerful inventions must not fall into the wrong hands." Strong hands forced her off in the wrong direction.

Olivia was about to scream when two guards from the facility appeared on the path. One guard seized the intruder, flailing and shouting, "Down with the patriarchy!"

A feminist cell in the dessert. Olivia was surprised. Her feet carried her back to the facility, future intact, with the other guard following thirty meters behind.

So she was under surveillance twenty-four, seven. Or. She'd saved her own life, through a new awareness. These seemed the most likely of many realities available for the calling.

In her suite, she sorted her belongings with alacrity. After putting things away, she opened the windows and lit sage. Smoke wafted into the shower and closets. Room fumigated, she was finished.

Earth

Thousands of years ago, the Greeks and Romans named the planets after gods and goddesses, Mercury, Venus, Mars, Jupiter, Saturn, Uranus, Neptune and Pluto. They named our own planet. We are supposed to know to worship the goddess Terra.

THE WORLD EVOLUTIONARY CONGRESS warmed up with Moroccan couscous and an accompaniment of belly dancers. Olivia wore her stunning gold and white evening gown. She was told the lamé hugged her curves like a glove.

After the exclusive dinner, the rest of the introverted scientists were invited out of their labs to join the international attendees for a breath of culture. The climax was a poetry slam commencing with 'A Cougar's Guide to Busting Arab Buns'. A challenger called it a cheap shot, though it did raise awareness above ripping off depressed tourists.

Olivia scanned the White-House-to-Wall-Street crowd. Most found the show vastly entertaining. Several with red faces and necks were looking forward to some real fun later. She was careful not to make eye contact with anyone. She searched for Axel's tall figure as the rappers battled on. A skinny poet was rocking, 'Why Perfect Partners are Sexy', when she realized Axel must be busy elsewhere.

Rumors were circulating that another three moguls had been forced to reconnect with the planet overnight. The corporate chieftains had been found growing peacefully in their rooms, eyelids seamed shut, aerial roots probing for moisture, company secrets locked away under mahogany skin. Around the mobile phone of one, a burl had formed. Dark green patches on both heels had sprouted and groped the floor for Earth.

Olivia avoided expectant eyes. There would be no cure. She called it a night and went back to her suite. She climbed into bed with her gold and white gown on.

In fitful sleep, she was walking toward Khalid. The evening was cool in the desert. His hands caressed, arms encircled her. Beard against chin, he drew her closer in a fierce embrace.

"Gentle," she pleaded.

The kiss, at last, her gown flapping like a flag. Gown piling onto the sand. Losing her balance, her body swayed into his chest. Strong arms tightened and held her to the mast. They centered, somewhere between her tummy and his hips. She felt him harden, press against her. Her leg lifted as they swayed in a dance. Her hand, revealing, stroking. He held her waist, turning her around, "*Ah, oui, this is what I want.*" He lowered her onto the sand and opened her thighs, weighing into the gold.

She received him with all her being. As he filled her, their needs dropped away. Entwined, understanding, one thrust from him, an answer from her, on top of him now, his eyes holding hers. He thrust, she thrust, echoing back and forth, swimming in each other's eyes for an eternity.

Honey.

False Top

Love as the negative or feminine ray, is content and ever seeks to enfold. Wisdom as the positive, masculine ray, is restless and always in pursuit. The feminine forces are ever striving to encircle the atom, and the masculine forces striving to propel it in a straight line. From this dual action of spiritual potentialities is born the 'Spiral', the motion of life and symbol of eternal progression.

— *Thomas Burgoyne*, Light of Egypt

ON THE DAY of the press conference, a knock came at her door. She looked through the peephole and recoiled at the sight of Faucheux. Her hands shook with rage. "What is it?" she demanded without opening.

"The Consortium requires your presence."

Time was up. She weighed her freedom against the man. The only hope lay in acquiescence. She mustered her poise, grabbed her briefcase, and avoided eye contact. No 'long time no see,' not even a handshake. Luckily, he'd taken on the local habit of walking ten paces ahead.

The autumn afternoon had been transformed with an unseasonable swelter. In the auditorium, members of the board were peeling off layers of clothing. You could never tell how to dress these days. Photographers and TV cameramen crowded around her at the door and followed her to the stage.

Olivia got a familiar feeling in the pit of her stomach as they passed the front row. A memory of Axel's smell piqued her intuition. She could feel him nearby. But scanning the crowd, she didn't see his head sticking out. What would he think of her now? She knew if she brought up his betrayal again, he'd just meet her gaze with those bewildered blue pools. She could still hear that British accent, "Do you think I *lied* to you?"

"We're too close to lie to each other. I would know." And she did. But confronting him would have meant losing him. He lied because he could, as an expression of his freedom. Because all he could see was the illusion of power over her. Whereas people who lied, let life play them, masking sacred truth, dealing out a trash heap of irrelevance, loss of respect, boredom, unnecessary byproducts of...un-love. Now she could see why they made it to the top. Because it wasn't the top.

The audience was full of men, but none was Axel. Reporters fired off questions she couldn't begin to answer. She passed the VIPs and overheard the board members talking.

"We should have given it to the man," one said. "She better have it."

Registering his tone, Olivia broke into a cold

sweat.

"They both almost had it when we started," the other member said. "Of course she's got it."

"If she doesn't, I know who can bleed it out of her."

The words slapped her in the face. Her feet felt numb as she climbed the steps to the stage, mind racing through the horrors they could employ to extract the loveoid formula from her...*don't give in to fear*. To come this far with the only plan, not having a plan. *All possibilities exist.* She wished she could jump tracks to another timeline. Olivia turned around at the podium. Axel was not present.

An elderly gentleman whistling his S's welcomed the members of the audience. Watching his waxed mustache, Olivia's knees began to wobble. He called her to the mic. Cameras flashed like popcorn. She had to lean on the podium to keep from losing her balance.

Faucheux stood behind her. She could feel his eyes on her back, seeing her through the lens of his own inadequacy. Her hands shook as she arranged her papers. The hopelessness of the situation weighed her tongue down. "It's a great honor to be here today." The spectators focused on Olivia. Her voice caved, and all that came out was a small whisper. "Thank you all for your support on the development of the loveoid." She kicked herself for coming to this point without a plan, and just watched the cameras flashing. *The moment when energy slows to the speed of light, and converts to matter.* The cameras sparkled like the waves on the sea in the sunlight. *To realize consciousness flows through all life around and in you, is enlightenment.* The flashes brought back her voice. All she could think of was thanking the exhaustive list of people who had made her research possible.

Next, she thanked Faucheux, and those who'd sabotaged her experiments.

A nervous, high-pitched laugh from the third row.

"...and I'd like to thank Shiva and Shakti, and also God."

She stepped back, eyeing the entrance. A tall figure waited in the doorway like a tree. Axel.

Her ears burned. She hoped he was over his colossal misfortune. Olivia looked at him squarely in the eye. Her opposite, identical in Nature, different in degree, stared back. She could tell he understood she was in danger; he'd heard the desperation in her voice. Hadn't he told her, a setback was one step closer to success. The world always attacked and frustrated rising women. You had to pick yourself up, and turn the experience to your advantage.

The press followed her gaze. Many recognized Axel, standing there scratching his chin. A murmur went around the room.

Olivia collected her papers. Let them screw themselves. Her soul wouldn't let her deliver a fake loveoid. Not for seven billion, not for prizes or titles.

Axel was the man for the job. His irreverence for the truth was exactly the quality she needed right now. If anyone could spin a yarn that would buy her some time, it was Axel.

Here goes. Olivia summoned all her power, and said in a strangled voice, "I will now give the floor to my colleague, an expert in the environment that the mutation strikes. Axel Harrington."

A few stragglers came in and pulled the door shut behind them. It hit Axel in the butt, and he stumbled into the room.

The front row chattered. "Of course, she couldn't do it alone."

"Eh bien?" Faucheux stiffened, unable to move for fear of letting on that things had just slipped out of control. The show must go on.

The audience fidgeted in their seats. Complaints were aired. As she walked along the stage, she overheard one board member say, "No one really expected the woman to do it without help."

Expectant eyes fell on the Brit, not especially dressed for the occasion, but on second glance, confidently disrespectful in faded jeans and a casual white T-shirt, tight around muscular arms.

She'd settle for one of his tailored lies.

A smattering of applause left Axel no choice. He walked forward, as Olivia stepped down. But their paths didn't cross. Instead, she stopped and shook his hand nervously, uttering between her teeth, "Do your thing. Obfuscate!"

"What's going on?" he demanded, holding onto her shaking hand.

One thing she liked about Axel, he always had money. "The loveoid's yours. I'll take your cash."

Axel straightened, chest expanding. The toast had landed butter-side up. He reached into his pocket. "Anything else?"

"Since you asked, I need time."

He rolled his eyes. "They told me who you were with these last few months. What's next, Olivia, a saber-toothed tiger?"

Olivia inspected her fingernails.

Faucheux's voice sounded in the mic. "And now, Dr. Axel Harrington. Dr. Harrington, would you step up to the podium?"

Axel's blue eyes held onto hers. "They're *grands seducteurs*. Don't accept any wooden nickels." He pulled out a wad of real money. Olivia leaned close as he passed her the bills discreetly.

She stuffed the cash between her papers. "Try to get beyond your stereotypes."

He scoffed.

"Just tell them about one of your pranks. Go into your project," she said, voice cracking. "Make it opaque."

"I got this," Axel said, an impish look on his face.

The prankster. Always ready to pull another fast one. She mouthed the word 'bye'.

Eyes widening, he hissed, "Go. Go, and don't come back!"

With that, Olivia inched up the aisle to the last row. Leaning against the wall, she waited for the cadence of Axel's baritone to settle into the loudspeakers. "Sorry for my tardiness. I'm very proud to be speaking to the love void today." His reassuring voice satisfied the audience. "I'd love, love to say I was finishing one last experiment, but to be honest, I was just stuck in traffic."

The room erupted into laughter. She caught one last look at him, trapped inside the body of an adult, pivoted on her heel, and tipped out the door.

Olivia dashed across the front lawn and out to the road. Waving a fifty-dinar note at the gardener, she asked for a lift to the sea.

He seemed to consider the possibility.

She took out another note. "Hurry!"

They got in the lawn truck. The gardener talked as he drove. She had to turn to the window so he couldn't see her transfer the money to her pocket. They bounced along.

"There!" Olivia pointed to a camel path leading out to a cliff. The gardener swerved the four-wheel-drive Citroen over the curb to the shortcut. He guided the jalopy through the underbrush, keeping to the remains of a dirt road. Thistle scratched at the sides of the truck as it bumped along the path. It lurched in and out of ditches. They finally alighted on a cliff overlooking the sea. The sun had descended, silhouetting the craggy rock. Olivia opened the door and ran to the tip of the escarpment. Warm wind swept her hair and skirt.

The gardener's eyes widened in horror. He jumped out of the truck.

But she stopped at the cliff edge. She opened her briefcase and took out her black box with all of the versions of the loveoid. She turned it upside-down and dumped everything over the cliff. The pills hit a jagged rock, and scattered into the waves. Then she threw the box off the cliff.

"What are you doing?" the gardener yelled, inching forward as you do when you're afraid someone might jump.

"Human's are the real pandemic, but no one's buying a pill for that." She took the lab results with the chemical, fig and dirt experiments out of her briefcase and tossed them into the ravine. The pages wafted into the crag. A gust of salty air blew her hair in all directions. She breathed it in. "Nature can take it from here." Then she turned on her heel.

"That's it, come back, Miss."

To the gardener's relief, Olivia took out another bill and said, "Now to Hôtel Dido."

"Normally it costs more than that."

"Alright."

He started the engine. They bumped along.

"I don't accept that doctors should be allowed to

euthanize," he said. "What if someone has an illness that's curable?'"

"Like meaningless work?"

"Ha! You're right. There's no cure for that."

Particles and Waves

Matter cannot be measured.

THE SOUL OF THE MEDITERRANEAN town exhaled; in the streets leading away from the cliff, harsh Nature struggled against Alexandrian ruin. The smattering of coastal hotels upheld an air of progress, though the tribal subconscious persevered.

The old neighborhood was cast in amber. They rolled through the familiar alleyways. Olivia had watched fortune unite couples here, and consume hopes. She was a different person now, ready to give the last of her energy. The seaside could lift the spirit, and humans could trample it in the next hour: all depended on the design of fate.

Haze hovered on the horizon. "It won't be long till the storm gets here," the gardener said. The *ch'hilli* sandstorm from the Sahara had already devastated Libya. The tropical air mass was pulled northward by low-pressure cells. Whether you considered its energy or matter, the storm travelling at a hundred kilometers an hour was enough to cause abrasion in metal. The gardener deposited her in front of Hôtel Dido.

Sparkling new front doors graced the lobby,

which had been painted lime green. The doorman greeted Olivia. A cleaning woman smiled and waved at Olivia, unsure of what to say. She couldn't exactly ask for a room.

A new Latif at the reception was glad to see her again. "With this flood of guests, we could use your help."

"Happy to oblige."

Olivia took the kit of drugs and passkey to the terminal wing.

She headed for the end of the long hallway in the hopes of finding an empty room to lie down in. The sandstorm had hit. She approached the brown view at the end of the hallway. She held her breath and closed the window against the dust.

Calm restored. The striped wallpaper clung to the corridor as always. Her work was done; no more lessons to learn.

She tried the last door on the left. A young man in a hospital gown looked up from his bed, eyes welcoming his perfect partner.

She stumbled backward into the hallway. She tried the door on the right: also full. There were no empty rooms! An old man occupied the bed. His breathing rasped. He seemed to be in a great deal of pain. The man opened his eyes. "I remember you," he said.

Mosfiloti, from the Mayor's barbecue. His bones protruded.

Sand blew in from the open window. Olivia set her kit on the nightstand, and went over to close the window. Dust blanketed all of the surfaces.

Mosfiloti called her to his bedside. "You'll be the daughter I never had." He rambled on about his childhood, gripping her hand, leading this new daughter into the thicket of adolescence, with its embarrassments and a veneer of regrets. His words were stifled by shocks of pain. "It's the best way out," he repeated over and over.

Olivia's clothes were suddenly too hot. Although she'd talked to many terminal guests and dissected many afterwards, she'd never actually euthanized anyone herself. "I don't know if I can do this," Olivia said. She shrank back at the thought of bad karma keeping her tethered to the planet. She didn't want to come back on a polluted Earth.

"I guarantee it's the right thing. I beg of you. I always knew it. Remember Osho's saying, 'Death can be made a celebration; you just have to learn how to welcome it, relaxed, peaceful.' "

"OK," she said. "We're doing this world a service." She hesitated a little before reaching for the red and yellow capsule. The stoic expression on her face softened. Sweat gathered on her upper lip. "It's better this way," she said, giving the old man the capsule. She poured him a cup of water from a water bottle. "You'll fall into a deep sleep."

"Thank you, daughter." His hand shook as he

took the cup. He stared at it for a full minute. Olivia put her arm around him.

Now she could see his true self emerging from all the fear. As helpless as he was in his bed, she recognized his grace. He put the capsule in his mouth and withdrew into a self-contained luminosity. She held his gaze as he swallowed it. A look of relief on his face, his eyes slowly closed. He relaxed into the pillows.

Mosfiloti slipped from his body. He centered as a being of pure energy, striving toward the white light.

Outside, the sky had turned brown. The wind blew a strange dust through the cracks in the windows. She'd heard it was full of asbestos from Syrian buildings being bombed since the start of the climate wars.

Olivia imagined she felt Mosfiloti's soul rising through the dust up to the ceiling, perhaps fusing with plasma in the atmosphere. She felt blessed. She was doing something purposeful with her knowledge.

Her life was complete. Even if she hadn't recognized love when it looked her in the eye.

Khalid. Without our bodies, we travel at the speed of thought.

She reached in her pocket and took out the small bottle of capsules. Looking at the dead man's solemn face, she wondered if her own soul was ready to access a high level. Perhaps killing out of compassion was the last lesson. She feared she still had more lessons to learn, and hoped Earth would remain habitable. She prayed for Mosfiloti, for Khalid, for herself, for the end to her bond with Earth.

She lifted her feet onto the bed next to Mosfiloti, and reached for the cup of water. "Let me discover life on another planet."

Khalid's face filled her thoughts. Love was real. They had cared, for a time. Love was fleeting. Only memory endured, until the remembrance of love couldn't keep you alive any longer. She had exhausted her life. She was ready.

Footsteps pounded down the hallway outside. She'd forgotten to lock the door!

It opened.

"Khalid!" *Alive!*

The yellow backpack on his back, Khalid stumbled through the doorway.

"Oh, thank God."

LOVEDIM

How Arab Lovers Are the Answer
to World Peace

*Oneness burst into pieces, expanding the outward proof of
its depth, observing chaos into life.*

"MOSFILOTI!" Khalid rushed to the bedside and held
his hand in front of the old man's nose. No breath
came out. "He was a nice man. Your work?"

"He was in pain." She released a deep sigh. "I
finally did something useful."

"You've done everything for me, and there's more
to do." Khalid gathered her into his arms. "That's all
there is. The rest is an illusion." He opened her hand.
The second red and yellow capsule lay among the
lines in her palm.

Crashing onto his shore, "Khalid—"

"I'm here." His arms encircling her, his face taut,
in earnest. "I want to die in your arms."

"What are you saying? You're too young. You
have a lot of love."

He studied the old man's peaceful face. Tears
welled in Khalid's dark eyes. "We'll live in the
whole spectrum. We don't have to see everything
black and white."

She smiled. "Even though I'm in bed with another

man?"

The look of victory on his face turned to incredulity at the thought. He cast a sportive frown at her. "*Salope!* I'll punish you."

She hugged and kissed him. Resting her head on his shoulder, she said, "I love you so much, Khalid. You saved my life again. I was ready to end it all."

"A permanent solution to a temporary problem."

"But Khalid, they'll kidnap us to get their dumb formula."

"We'll run. I have water in my backpack. We'll take the ferry to Egypt. It's Wednesday. We have two days."

Olivia cocked her head. Shouts echoed outside the window.

She grabbed his arm.

"Run!" He pulled her off the bed.

With one last look at Mosfiloti, they ducked down the corridor. Khalid kicked a security door open.

The sandstorm was amassing power. They fled toward the bush.

The red horizon glowered at them. Dust blew in their faces. Olivia stole a look back. A commotion was erupting outside the hospital, uniformed men scurrying into a white van. It veered out of the driveway in pursuit. "They're coming!"

Khalid grabbed Olivia's hand. "Let's get off the road." The storm stirred up the desert floor. They couldn't see their feet. She glanced at the fugitive sun. He led her over an embankment, deeper into the dust cloud. Khalid tied his shirt around his nose and mouth. Olivia pulled her scarf over her face to keep the sand from blowing into her lungs.

Bushes gave way to tumbleweeds as they ran deeper into the storm. The wind covered their tracks. Khalid escaladed an embankment and slid down the other side. The uniformity of the desert awakened Khalid's blindsight. He changed their trajectory, zigzagging toward a newly formed dune.

The sand pelted Olivia's face and forced her to walk with her eyes closed. She tried to call his name, but got a mouthful of wind. Once in a while, she squinted to pinpoint Khalid, visible intermittently up ahead, then closed her eyes tight again. She watched her eyelids. A bright dot pulsated in a screen of black. It gave way to splotches of color. With the ongoing rhythm of her feet, the blots came into focus. She could see. Veins of energy budded, flowered and were consumed as if by fire. The seed of life.

She walked on. The numbness in her legs spread till she couldn't feel the rest of her body. The sand hit her face. The dunes blurred, and her eyes shut again. *Everything is and isn't, at the same time.* All at once, a rocket launched in her head, and she lurched forward. She fell down a shaft — minus one, minus two, minus three — but after the lowest energy center, she missed hitting the ground. All was blissfully calm, as if she'd become a wave.

Pulsating in her mind's eye, was a vague sense of herself on the horrible day of the attack in the hotel lobby. But this time, she was standing outside the hotel lobby, with the palm trees. Astonished at the magnetism of the palm trees, she leaned into their field, merging with them and feeling profoundly in the moment, as if creating another future. Together, they observed the waves of her former self into matter.

Materializing fully now, her former self took the envelope from the concierge, then looked out the window in the direction of her present self.

Khalid and the other worker walked by. She watched her former self drop the paper on the floor. But instead of bracing herself for what came next, an incredible feeling of love overflowed from her heart to her former self. Suddenly, the flow of events leading up to the present collapsed into the eternal now. Her two selves' history became visible all at once, painted as a symbol.

She was shaking, tears streaming from closed eyes. For the first time in her life, Olivia was utterly happy to be alive. They were going to Egypt, and she wanted nothing more than this moment in this desert. Her energy pulsated outward. Now she saw. An array of possibilities blew in the wind. The problems emerging were, in fact, the very stepping stones for creating a future.

The shaking stopped. Her weight felt impossible to move. Her eyes opened. The storm was gaining momentum. Golden particles sparkled in the air, a fork in the path. The desert lay before her in a galaxy of stardust. Beyond these tiny suns, her man's silhouette appeared, traipsing across a dune toward freedom.

Olivia's body crystallized around her flame. She picked herself up.

The Right Fork

Reality is and isn't. The most basic particles can be in a 1 or 0 quantum state. But as waves, they can also be in a superposition of the 1 and 0 states. However, when they are measured, the result is always either a 1 or a 0; the probability of an 'is' or 'isn't' outcome depends on the consciousness of the quantum state they were in.

DELIVERANCE CAME at the final moment when night requites day. They stood together on a dune, a discontinuous transition from one place to another, without going through the space in between.

A mound was poking out of the next dune up ahead. A gust of sand, and it wasn't. As they slid down, the mound appeared again. It grew bigger. At the bottom, the dust cleared, revealing the remnants of another era. The still life was wedged into the drift. They walked toward the ruin. It appeared and disappeared behind clouds of sand.

A goatherd's hut cropped out of a dried patch of underbrush. A primitive life came at them all at once. There was no way to step into the scene and continue believing in time.

Khalid led Olivia through the doorway into the one room that was still standing. Olivia swooned.

He held the water bottle to her mouth. Then he took one sip himself.

"I'm so glad you're alive."

"We're married now."

They were, and they weren't at the same time. What matter, the world disintegrating around them...

*

The Moon had transited the sky. Were they dozing? A past forgotten. Relaxing into the slowest vibration, his fingers stretched across her middle, and awoke her breasts. "Some fear love is death. We know it." He fixed her against him in the sign of a cross. Bodies sweating, thighs hot molten time, he was back inside her temple.

A silent thunder reverberated, banishing her self, inviting her opposite. Had there been another woman? From the intersection of their hips, a younger waif rolled out like a rug over Olivia's body, becoming her. Olivia glanced down at her own stomach, but instead saw the other woman's slight frame lying in her place. *How can this be?* Amazed at her duality, Olivia scrutinized the woman's thin ribs with curiosity, a little God trying to see Itself. Gazing at the desert blossom's slight waist, Olivia was even more surprised to feel no jealousy at all for her other pole; to be sacrificing for love, surrendering her self, *I am the other woman.*

The moment Olivia glanced at Khalid, the other woman split off to the left, thin body mingling with the moonsheen on the wall, then escaping to another parallel. Had Khalid noticed the other woman? The irony of Olivia's sacrifice. He was entirely transfixed on her face.

His eyes seized hers. Now he was inside Olivia. She caught her breath, astonished at the transformation in her lover. Moonlight illuminated the face of a God. Serious at work, male power gazed at her display naked on the ground, bathing in his glory. *She* was his universe. His broad hands spread her on the dirt. She took in his divine face, unity of energy and matter, seen and unseen in silvery light, hair glowing with moment. Exquisite features chiseled an expression of authority. *Now it's me he's inside.* Proof of God, pumping in earnest and creating possibility for an impossible love to go on through the spectrum of being. *I am the ground beneath us I am the Moon shining through the roof and the fire in your eyes the path of the sun I am the drumming of the tides the wind on the sea I am the vessel and also the lightning striking the vessel.*

Observers

When they are observed, electrons are 'forced' to behave like particles and not like waves. Thus the act of observation affects the experimental findings.

WITH A CLAP of thunder, the desolating sandstorm blew through the desert. The life occupying it wasn't, and it was.

At the first hint of dawn, a fennec fox poked his bat ears out of a hole. His nose sniffed the clean air outside the hut.

Eyes half-closed, a sand lizard froze at the sound of a helicopter. The hum grew louder until it beat on the dunes and sent fennec, lizard, and all wilderness observers undercover.

The chopper advanced toward the mound. Hovering over the hut, the machine stirred up new torrents of wind. The pilot set off a flare.

Six minutes later, a jeep carrying two stretchers climbed the dune and stopped. A team of barking dogs jumped out and slid down in an avalanche of sand. Four men aimed their automatics at both the entrance and the window of the hut. Two more slid down and pulled the remains of the door away. They went in. Sand cascaded across the threshold.

The dogs wagged their tails. They sniffed the air, and sneezed.

Funeral Pyre

Everything is in the eye of the beholder.

THE MOAN OF A SAXOPHONE lingered on the *naseem* breeze. Purple sky waited between the branches.

A drum answered.

The funeral-goers stood up. The sax ripped out further enticement, luring the crowd onto the path. The music was astonishingly uplifting for a funeral, inviting everyone to go with the flow.

Welcoming smiles. Nothing wrong with being happy — once you could enjoy sadness, you were neither; you were beyond your emotions, aware and unaware, celebrating both: the oneness of truth and the veil to the beyond.

A dancer brandishing a tambourine led the whirling. People skipped and trotted, brimming with joy. Cheers rang out. The festivities at Hôtel Dido had begun.

An old woman clenched the railing as she hobbled down the shadowy steps of the euthanasia hotel. She was muttering, "Sad, sad." She stopped and looked up at the sky. Her sceptical look met the gaze of a seven-foot scientist, who seemed to be in charge, and she decided to have a word with him. "Another funeral," she called over the fray.

"To some." It depended on how you saw it.

"Well, you don't usually *celebrate* youth passing to the beyond."

The scientist was scratching his chin. "It's not as common."

Looking into his blue eyes, the woman forgot her complaint, and had a vague feeling she'd been tricked. "I guess sadness isn't so bad."

"It has its beauties." Axel stopped to feel the depth of the darkness. A place of velvet silence within the din. At least sadness wasn't shallow. He watched the yin of the half Moon as it waxed over the bubbling celebration. As long as you remained the observer, becoming neither darkness nor light, everything could be celebrated.

Laughing and singing behind twin coffins, a harangue of red-robed figures paraded down the hill, arms extended to the sky above Hôtel Dido. The river of funeral dancers jiggled along the path after them. An elderly troop followed amidst scarves floating on the breeze.

Eight veiled worshippers carried the coffins onto the beach. The fanfare streamed behind in a torrent of laughter and music. People stacked logs on the funeral pyre around the coffins. Creased hands pressed together in prayer. Then, the people held hands in a big circle and hummed. When both coffins were secure in their places, a priest set a torch to the kindling. The fire crackled. Flames stripped off the calculus of time. Energy rose. Waves lapped at the shore, ablaze.

The sea watched, an orange reflection of plasma.

Parallelly

Where hate leaves off and love begins.

THE BUSH RUSTLED with wildlife watching from their camouflage. Feet trod past in single file.

Robed in sunlight, the lovers traipsed on. Several paces ahead, Khalid carried the yellow pack. Blind determination had displaced the wherewithal to communicate. Sand cascaded downward as they forced their exhausted selves up another dune.

Though their minds were always on Sol, they kept their squinting eyes fixed on their footsteps to navigate the shifting sands, and avoid sliding downward.

The sun climbed higher.

At the top of the tallest dune yet, they stopped. His arm reached for the curve of her sunburnt waist.

Beneath them lay the port, lined with cafés and souvenir shops. White ships dotted the gleaming water, and in their midst floated the MV Ptolemy, still sailing through war and pandemic. The second-class cruise ship was one tough hulk.

Serenity beckoned.

A howl of laughter echoed through the desert.

They slid down the dune, arms wide. Legs supple,

glissading toward the port, amidst grains of sand, shards reflecting the sun, *glanced two shards, always one.*

**More books from
Harvard Square Editions**